END

OF THE

ROAD

END
OF THE
ROAD

ZEATA P. RUFF

YAV PUBLICATIONS

ASHEVILLE, NORTH CAROLINA

Cover Illustration by Zeata P. Ruff.
Cover print available for purchase at GrinsAndGigglesArt.com

First Edition

ISBN: 978-1-937449-20-9

Published by:

YAV PUBLICATIONS
ASHEVILLE, NORTH CAROLINA

YAV books may be purchased in bulk
for educational, business, or promotional use.
Contact Books@YAV.com or phone toll-free 888-693-9365.
Visit our website: www.InterestingWriting.com

3 5 7 9 10 8 6 4 2

Assembled in the United States of America
Published April 2013

For "Big Jim" who would not let me quit.

TABLE OF CONTENTS

THE CRAWFORD FAMILY TREE
1949

MORT
Age 19

ANDY
Age 17

MAGGIE
Age 16

MATT
Age 14

BETTY
Age 12

JOE
Age 11

LIL' JIM
Age 10

R.L. CRAWFORD - Father
Daddy Robert - R.L.'s Father
Mama Annie - R.L.'s Mother

VADIE CRAWFORD- Mother
Granny Ruth - Vadie's Mother

CHAPTER 1

WESTERN NORTH CAROLINA MOUNTAINS

NOVEMBER, 1949

THEY SLIPPED IN, all five of them, kinda like they were hopin' nobody would notice. Set on the back row. But folks did notice. First one, then another, then somebody would elbow his neighbor so they'd turn around. The church was almost full, nigh on fifty people. It sounded like a bunch of bees had done and got loose with all the buzzin'. Nobody was payin' any mind as to what the preacher was a sayin'. All five of the latecomers, except Big Jack, was lookin down at their shoes like they'd never seen 'em before. Just waitin' for somebody to tell 'em they weren't welcome here. But Big Jack was sittin' up real straight like he was still in the army and just darin' somebody to say something.

It's the first time that they'd been to church since...and I don't recollect that I've ever seen Big Jack in church. Preaching and singing went on—just like always. But you could see folks takin' a peek over their shoulder ever now and again, makin' sure they was seeing what they was seeing. All five sneaked out just as the preacher was passin' their row to stand at the door. Reckon they knew what all the whispering was about. Everybody else was singin' the last hymn.

"Hazel, wait!" Mama called kinda loud, as she squeezed between me and my friend, Harvey. She stepped out into the church aisle just as we finished up the last verse. "Wait, Hazel," she called again and rushed to the back of the church almost knocking Miz Henderson back down in her pew. Mama brushed by the preacher without even a howdy, still hollerin at Hazel Hall to stop.

The whole Crawford clan was right behind her, falling all over themselves and trying to figure out what Mama was gonna do. Ain't never seen Mama act like that or run that fast—and in church, too. Pa stopped, but just for a minute, and helped Miz Henderson steady her feet. "Sorry, Fannie, don't know what's got into Vadie."

"R.L., you all go ahead and get in the truck. I won't be but a minute. I gotta speak to Hazel," Mama hollered back over her shoulder just as we got outside. We couldn't do nothing but just stand there and watch Mama runnin across the grass toward the Halls. "Please wait, Hazel!"

When I looked back at the church door, it seems like everybody had come out all at once. Pushed their way right past the preacher. Their mouths all gapped open and not takin' their eyes off of Mama. They watched as she ran over to Miz Hall and put her hand on her shoulder, "Please wait a minute, Hazel. I need a word with you," Mama begged almost out of breath.

Hazel Hall stopped but kept her head bowed and didn't look Mama in the face. She turned around, kinda slow like. The Hall boys and Big Jack stepped up real close behind her, like they weren't sure what was goin' to happen or what Mama could possibly have to say. Reckon nobody did, cause the churchyard was soon full of gawkin' folks and nobody sayin a word. They were all strainin' to hear what Mama could possibly have to say to Hazel Hall.

"Glad to see you and your boys back at church, Hazel. You, too, Big Jack," Mama began and she sorta nodded at each one and caught her breath. "Been real tough on all of us these last few weeks. I finally came around to realizing that God and church are the only way to get through it. You're a good woman, Hazel, and got some real fine boys here. Nothing for you to hang your head about. No need for these boys to be feeling ashamed either. Had nothing to do with it."

"But, Vadie...how can you of all people forgive...." Hazel stammered, a tear rolling down her cheek.

"You listen to me. There's nothing to forgive. It hasn't been easy—on any of us. I'm sure that there'll still be some dark days ahead but I've turned it over to the Lord and I know He'll take care of it. Good Book says that the Lord don't put nothing on us that we can't handle. Took me a while, but I finally remembered that I'm a mountain woman, made of strong faith and sturdy grit like my mama and a lot of the other women around these mountains. You are, too, Hazel, and don't you forget it. It's gonna be hard but we'll make it to the end of this road. We got to. Gotta do it for our young 'uns' sake. You've had a hard row to hoe for a long time, these boys, too. But you've made it through. So you hold your head high and don't let nobody tell you any different." Mama turned around and headed toward the truck leavin' Miz Hall and the rest of Shady Hill Baptist Church starin after her.

"I'm ready, now, R.L.," I heard her tell Pa as she climbed into the front seat. "You know, we got a lot to do and it's almost Thanksgiving," she added taking a long, white feather from the dashboard and rubbing it against her cheek. "Don't know when I've seen these Smokey Mountains look so clear on such cold November day."

It sure was gonna be good to have Mama back to her old self. Even if I am only 10 years old, I know that 1949 was a hard year and things could only get better. Had to. For all of us. What began back in January maybe ended today. Mama let Miz Hall and the rest of Hazelgrove know.

CHAPTER 2

JANUARY 1949—THE LIST

IT WAS KINDA WARM for a January day. Yesterday's rain had frozen last night but had been thawed by the morning sun to make a slick layer of gooey, brown slush. The river of mud was covering the whole dog lot. Saturday chores were getting done but nobody was movin' fast. It was nice just to let the let the sun warm your bones as you worked.

"Joe, you and Lil' Jim rake that lot out real good afore you put down fresh straw. We'll move Queenie to the porch tomorrow, but I want that lot clean for Napoleon," Pa yelled at us from the back porch.

"Don't he see we're working as hard as we can? Don't know why he's in such a bad temper. Got the longest list he's ever had. I think he's still mad about Brother Mort joinin' up last week," I complained to Joe.

"Y-y-yeah," Joe replied. "We're w-w-workin' h-h-hard."

Sometimes Joe has a hard time getting his words out just right. He talks kinda funny and kids make fun. Sometimes he don't talk at all, especially if they's strangers around. One time, I heard his teacher tell another teacher that Joe was "slow". But heck, he ain't slow. He can run faster than anybody in 5th grade.

"Matt, bring me some more of them shavins out of the barn!" Pa yelled again. "Here, Andy, make sure that box is snug in the corner and there ain't no nails or nothing stickin out. It's gonna turn cold and we'll need to keep 'em out of the weather." They shoved the large wooden box that Andy had just built, back into the far corner of the back porch. It was ready to be filled with the cedar shavings that would keep Queenie and her new born pups warm.

"Get on in your house, Napoleon, and stay out of the way!" I ordered, a little bit ticked off. About every other year, it seems like the whole world turns around Pa's list. Don't nothin else matter. Gotta take care of Queenie! Make sure Queenie has plenty of food. Queenie got plenty of straw in her house. Queenie this, Queenie that! Guess that dog thinks she really is some kind of Queen.

Pa started raising bird dogs afore I was born. He's had some real dandies but none like Queenie. Bout three years back, they started havin' a contest over in Asheville just for bird dogs. Guess they got tired of every hunter sayin' his dog was better than yourn and no way to prove it. So they come up with this here contest—call it field trials. Have it in September and everybody brings all their dogs together and watches 'em work. They judge 'em on their find and point, and on their retrieve. They even judge 'em on how they look—their color and markins' and such. Well, Pa's been takin' Queenie ever since they started and ever year she comes back with another little tag on her collar "BEST OF SHOW." Must really be something, 'cause ever since, Pa's list has got longer and longer.

Now, Napoleon, here, well he was the runt of Queenie's first litter. So small, nobody thought he would make it. But he's also the meanest of the litter. When he was hungry, which seemed like most of the time, he'd root his brothers and sisters out of the way until he could latch on and git his fill. That's why they named him 'Napoleon'. It was Brother Mort's idea. Seems like that there was this here King in France a long time ago who was real small but kinda mean. He had big armies and tried to rule the world. It sure is a funny name for a dog but I guess it fits.

"Hey, Joe, here comes the first uns!" I called as the two pickups drove up the driveway and stopped at the porch where Pa and Andy were putting the shavins in the box. "That's old man Snyder and his boy. Where are they on the list?"

"Don't know. M-m-must be-e-e near the t-t-top, though, 'cause they's here l-l-last week, too," Joe answered.

"Don't know them fellers in the other truck, do you?" I asked as they all began to make their way toward us sloshing through the mud. Each man put in a fresh chew and offered one to Pa just as they reached the gate.

"You keep a clean pen, R.L., that's real important," Mr. Snyder said as Pa lifted the hasp. Everybody else nodded in agreement. "How much longer you figure she's got?"

"Maybe a week, 10 days at the most. Me and my boy, Andy, are fixin' her a place on the back porch. She had a hard time with that last litter and we want to keep a close eye on her," Pa answered just as another truck pulled in behind the others. David Lee Hall and his oldest son, Johnny Lee, got out and started toward the group. The Halls are our only close-by neighbors. They have three boys. Johnny Lee, is 17 and one of the boys that likes my sister Maggie. Why, one Sunday, he was tryin' so hard to get her attention that he fell over his own two feet and landed right smack in the third row in old Miz Setzer's lap. She weren't none too happy and let him have an ear full right there in the middle of church. Johnny Lee just picked up his hat and ran out the door. He didn't say excuse me or nothin. Don't know where he was but he sure didn't come back to preachin' for a couple of Sundays.

"Hey, R.L., just the man we need to see!" David Lee yelled as he came up the hill. "Understand Queenie's bout due."

"You all know Fred Snyder and his boy, Carl. This here's Joe Hunter and Sam Fox. Our neighbor, David Lee Hall, and his boy, Johnny Lee," Pa made the introductions as the Halls joined the other men. Everybody shook hands and spit tobacco over their shoulder. It's kinda what all the men folk do around here to let everybody know that they's all on the same footin'.

"Well, R.L., me and my boy want one of them pups. I'll pay top dollar. Figure I just might git in the bird dog business myself," David Lee announced as he nodded to each man and spit again, barely missin Fred Snyder's boot.

Spittin' tobacco juice on the ground, and wippin his mouth on the sleeve of his coat, Pa took a minute to answer. "Your name ain't on the list, David Lee. Queenie probably won't have more than 7, maybe 8, and I already got eleven on the list. Everybody that don't get a pup this time will move up the list for the next litter."

"Hell, R.L., ain't we been neighbors a long time? Good neighbors. Don't reckon it would hurt nothin for you to put me on the top of the list and let somebody else wait, now would it?" he suggested as he patted Pa on the shoulder and spit once more, barely missing another boot.

"No, David Lee, it don't work that way. First come, first serve—that's how it's made. Don't move it around for nobody. Sides that, don't know as how I will put your name on the list for the next litter, either." Pa was quick to answer as he looked him right in the eye.

"Why, what do you mean? I got just as much right as anybody else! Ain't my money good enough for a Crawford?" he asked angrily, pushing the sleeves of his coat up like he was getting ready to fight. Everybody knows that David Lee Hall has a quick temper and likes to shove his weight around.

"It ain't your money, David Lee. It's the way you treat your dogs. Last fall, you kept a coon dog tied to a tree until it almost starved to death. A body could see his ribs poking out. Don't want my pups goin' to nobody that would mistreat 'em. You'll have to find 'em somewhere else if you want a dog." Turning to the other men, "Fred, you and Carl come back in about two weeks and y'all can git the pick of the litter. Your name's on the top."

"Come on, Pa," Johnny Lee quietly said to his father as he tugged on his sleeve and urged him toward their truck. It was easy to see that Johnny Lee was afraid that his Pa might start fightin' or something.

"Let go of me, Johnny Lee! Don't you ever put your hands on your Pa again, you hear!" David Lee growled and pushed his son into the mud. "Ain't no use tryin' to talk to 'em no ways. Shoulda knowed. He's a Crawford. Thinks he's better than everybody else. Hell, we'll show 'em. I'll just git me a dog and see who wins them trials the next time," David Lee yelled back to the group of stunned men as a red-faced Johnny Lee followed him toward the truck, head bowed and mud all over the knees of his pants. "You'll see! You'll see! Won't let no Crawford beat me."

As the father and son reached the truck, he grabbed Johnny Lee by the coat and shoved him into the side of the truck, "Don't you ever embarrass me like that again, boy, you hear? Don't need no snot-nosed kid telling me what to do. Now git in this here truck. I'll take care of you when we git to the house."

The other men milled around makin' small talk for a few minutes before they left, making sure to let David Lee get on down the road. Nobody could help but hear what he said to Johnny Lee and nobody wanted any more trouble.

Before the day was over, all the rest of the fellers on the list would stop by to check on Queenie.

"Why do you always want Queenie to litter in the middle of the winter, Pa?" I asked as we finished supper. "Wouldn't it be better if it was in the middle of the summer when it's hot and you don't have to check on her so much?"

"Yeah, Lil' Jim, it'd be OK anytime. But I like to have my pups ready early in the year so that their handlers can git some trainin' in before bird season in the fall. If they're eight or nine months old, you can put them in the field with the older dogs and they'll just fall right in—it's in their blood. They know just what they're suppose to do," he patiently explained. "Good supper, Mama."

"Nothin special," Mama answered, distracted, as she began to clear the table. "Wonder what Mort's havin?"

"Sh-h-h! Everybody be real quite. Listen, Pa. Ain't that Queenie and Napoleon?" Andy asked as we all held real still and strained to hear. "Bet that old fox is back, looking for something to eat."

"Well, he might git et hisself if he tries to git in Napoleon's food." Pa laughed as we all listened to the song of the barking dogs. "He's probably just passin' through. Listen, they've stopped. We'll move Queenie first thing in the morning. Don't need her all stressed out so near her time. Now, y'all git on in bed. We've had a hard day. Got a lot to do before church in the morning."

"Ah, Pa, I ain't sleepy. Let us listen to a little of the Opry afore we have to tuck in," Matt begged. "Little Jimmy Dickens is suppose to be on tonight."

"Yeah, Pa," everybody chimed in. "We'll go directly. Let us listen to it a little bit."

"You all heard me. Git on up them steps. Don't need nobody pitchin' a hissy fit. Been a long day. And don't forget to give your Mama some sugar afore you tuck in."

When Pa said something, he meant it and would never change his mind. So we all lined up to kiss Mama on the cheek afore climbing the stairs.

We began our chores just as the sun was peeking over the mountains. Pa had sent Andy to the dog lot to bring Queenie to her new spot on the back porch. "Pa, come quick! Come quick! Queenie's gone and something is wrong with Napoleon!" Andy yelled toward the house.

"What are you hollerin' about, Son?" Pa yelled back as he leaped off the porch and ran toward the lot. Betty hung her egg basket on the fence, Joe and I dropped our load of firewood and we all ran in the same direction.

"The gate was open, Pa! The gate was open! When I got here, the gate was open. Queenie ain't nowhere and Napoleon's layin' over there behind his house! I think he's dead! Pa." Andy shouted louder even though we were all standin right beside him.

"Let me look at Napoleon, git out of the way. Maybe he's just sick," Betty said through tears as she knelt beside the still dog.

"Queenie, here Queenie!" Pa called over and over as he wandered around the lot and up toward the pine trees. "Queenie, Queenie! Here girl!" But the dog did not appear.

"Ain't no way she coulda got out. Somebody had to flip the hasp and open the gate. Ain't no way," Andy said shaking his head and looking all around the frozen grounds.

"Joe, you and Lil' Jim go to the barn and see if she might be down there with Maggie and Matt. See if they've seen her. Maybe she got out and went down there last night to git warm."

"Pa, Napoleon is dead. He ain't breathin or nothing. Oh, Pa, what do you think coulda happened to Napoleon and Queenie?" Betty begged for an answer, tears streaming down her cheeks as she cradled the dog's head in her lap and rocked back and forth.

"We gotta find Queenie. She's too near her time to be out wanderin around. Now, git goin boys. Go on down to the barn and see if she's there. We'll take care of Napoleon later, Betty. Go tell your Mama that Queenie's missin. Here Queenie! Come here girl! Queenie!"

But she wasn't at the barn. She wasn't at the can house or the chicken coop or under the front porch. She was nowhere to be found. It took a while, but finally Pa understood what Andy was tryin to say, "Ain't no way she could unlock the gate. Somebody had to do it."

"Andy, take the truck down to the store and tell Daddy Robert to call the sheriff," Pa ordered. "The sooner he gits on this the sooner we have her back."

The sheriff drove up in his patrol car about nine o'clock looking none too pleased about having to come out this far on such a cold day and a Sunday to boot.

"Sheriff Taylor, you gotta find out who took my dog, Queenie. It's about her time and if she's not took good care of, she might lose those pups and not make it herself," Pa almost begged the sheriff.

"Look, R.L., I'm real sorry about your dog. But I don't have no time to go looking for strays. I got real sheriff work to do. We got us some Klan trouble. Last night somebody done burned a cross in old man Putnam's yard. I been up almost all night tryin' to figure out what's going on."

"What do you mean, Sheriff? We ain't never had no Klan around here. Why would anybody have a gripe with poor old Ned Putnam. He ain't never caused nobody trouble."

"I don't know, R.L. You remember his boy, Nathanial? Well, seems he moved back in with Ned a few weeks back. Been livin' down round Charlotte and got into some trouble with some white boys that didn't like the way he's talkin' to white girls. My guess is, he decided the these hills are a lot safer than that flat land. But I reckon somebody done found out and followed him up here," Sheriff Taylor explained to all the Crawford males who were staring in disbelief.

"That's mighty disturbin'. We don't need that kind of trouble around here. Maybe they've had their say and will let it be. I ain't seen Nathaniel around. How old is he now anyway? 15? 16? Think I remember he's about the same age as Andy?"

"Probably about 17," The sheriff answered. "He was just a little 'un when Ned sent him off to live with his mother-in-law."

"Guess Nathaniel has been layin' low. Best he stays holed up until this blows over," R.L. told him shaking his head and looking at his boys, who were as still as mice. Their mouths all gapped open. "You reckon it was men from down around Charlotte? Don't think they could be from around here."

"I hope they ain't from around here. I hope they are from Charlotte and are long gone. Gotta go, R.L. Hope you find your dog."

"But I'm tellin you, Queenie was stole. Stole right outta her lot. And who ever took her musta poisoned Napoleon, too. That's a crime—that's not a stray!" Pa tried to explain again as the sheriff got back into his car.

"It was that mean ole David Lee Hall! Up here yesterday trying to buy one of the pups. You otta stop by his place. Bet you'd find Queenie tied in his barn!" Andy yelled at the sheriff.

"Now don't go off half-cocked, Andy. Gotta have proof. I'll keep my eyes open, R.L. I'll keep my eyes open. If I turn anything up, I'll let you know. You let me know if you hear anything about this Klan stuff," and he drove out of our drive with us all looking at each other.

"What's the Klan, Pa?" I ventured to ask.

"Nothin' for you to trouble your head about, Lil' Jim. Not none of you. Just a bunch of men with hate in their heart instead of the love of the Lord. Think they know what's best, yet, they hide behind white robes and masks," he explained to his four dumbfounded sons. "Now, what we gotta do is find Queenie. Gotta find her before she pups and we lose her as well as her brood. Lil' Jim, you and Joe dig a grave for Napoleon. The rest of us will divide up and search for Queenie. You boys get a move on, you hear? Don't look like we'll be going to church."

"Bet it was that David Lee Hall. Came up here yesterday with his chest all stuck out wantin' to buy a pup. I wouldn't put nothing past him," Andy accused. "Probably got her tied up down at his barn right now. Come on, Pa, let's go down there and git her back!"

"I don't know, Andy. We can't go accusing somebody just because we don't like 'em. And we shore can't go down there and make a ruckus. But we'll watch and if you get a chance, ask Johnny Lee about it. He might just tell you—especially if his Pa's been beatin' on him again." Pa just shook his head and went into the house.

"Shucks, I gotta a good mind to go on down there myself—right now! Just see what old David Lee's got in that barn! Probably got Queenie and no telling what else," Andy told his brothers.

"Better not, Andy! Better just be quite about it and keep our eyes open, like Pa said," Matt stated and the rest of us nodded. "No telling what David Lee would do if he caught you sneakin' around. He may even be one of them Klan fellers."

"Yeah, he's real mean. He might even shoot you!" I added. "You saw what he did to Johnny Lee yesterday when he didn't do nothin but try to keep him from fightin!"

"Well, I ain't afraid. Ain't afraid of David Lee or the Klan or nobody. And I shore wouldn't let David Lee push me around like he did Johnny Lee. First time he hit me, I'd hit him back—right in the mouth. Pa or no Pa. Ol' David Lee acts real tough but I bet he ain't. Bet he's just bluffin'. Bet if somebody stood their ground, he'd tuck his tail and run like some scared pup. Be just like him to be one of them fellers hidin' behind some white robe and mask. Sneakin' around, afraid to show his face. But I won't go. I'll do what Pa said and ask Johnny Lee first time I see him. Tell him he better fess up if he knows what's good for him, too. Tell him we know his Pa's got Queenie and we'd better git her back! And her pups, too! And they'd all better be in good shape."

"Wh-o-o's that Nathaniel guy? Y-y-you kn-kn-know him, Andy?" Joe asked.

"Nah, I don't know him. You all know his pa. Colored man who works down at the mill, sweepin' up. And his ma works for some ladies in town, helping' with cleanin' and stuff. Real nice folks. Wonder why they sent him off? Maybe he's touched in the head or something," Andy answered his brother. "Maybe you and Lil' Jim better start lookin' over your shoulder when you're walking home."

"Come on Joe, lets finish diggin that grave and get Napoleon buried afore Betty gits back out here and starts bawlin' again," I said, picking up a shovel. Everybody scattered. If they're like me, gotta a lotta thinking to do.

At least the wet ground had thawed and the digging wasn't hard. I couldn't help but think about David Lee Hall as we shoveled the soggy dirt into a big pile. Don't know if Andy's right or not about his stealin Queenie...he sure seems mean enough. Can't figure about this Klan stuff, either. Sounds kinda scary. Sure wouldn't want to make them mad. Just glad that Andy didn't take it on hisself to go down to the Halls and stir up more trouble.

And that Nathaniel feller. Boy, I sure wouldn't like it if Ma and Pa sent me away to live with somebody else. Even if it was kin. "Joe, do you think Andy's right? About that colored feller being touched?" I asked as we dug.

"D-d-don't k-k-know about you, but I am gonna be careful," he answered. "D-d-don't want nobody s-s-sneakin' up on me. T-t-touched or not."

CHAPTER 3

FEBRUARY, 1949

"WAKE UP AND LOOK OUT THE WINDOW, JOE, it's snowin'!" I whispered. "Bet it's gonna be knee deep!"

"What ti..ti..ti..time is it, Lil' Jim?" Joe asked not wanting to open his eyes. Hadn't he just got in bed?

"I don't know. It's not daylight yet. Look, Joe, it's snowin' flakes bigger 'n saucers! The ground's already white. And look! You can't even see the mountains cause it's snowin' so hard. Yep, we're gonna get a good 'un," I whispered a little louder this time.

"Will you two shut up!" Matt grumbled. "You've both seen plenty of snow lots of times and we're gonna have to get up soon. Now git back to sleep!"

But I just couldn't stay in the bed. It's almost the end of February and this is the first snow to amount to anything we've got. So far, the winter of 1948-49 has been cold, wet, and rainy. The kind where you just want to stay inside, hunker down by the fire, listen to the radio or maybe read a book or work a jigsaw puzzle. But now, just look, finally, we were getting the snow that I love. Gazing out the window at the wonderful, white, wonderland, it was amazin' how everything could turn white so fast. Every small branch and blade of grass grabbed the flakes as they fell. Even the barbed wire fence held its narrow row of fluffy, white stuff. Wonder why it don't fall off, I pondered to myself as everybody else snuggled down in their beds.

The old house was quiet—it always seemed a lot more quiet when it snowed. The only sound was Pa's snoring' and everybody was used to that and it didn't keep nobody awake—not even Mama. Over in one corner of the bedroom, Matt and Andy were tangled up in their quilts tryin' to keep warm. Joe always hogged all the covers on our bed and caused many a tug-of-war in the middle of the night. Maggie and Betty were sound asleep in the next room and Brother Mort would have been asleep downstairs in the corner of the sitting room if he hadn't of gone to join up with the Army right after Christmas.

The quiet was broken. I could hear Mama in the sittin' room stokin' the fire in the Warm Morning Heater. Must be five o'clock. She always got up first and always made sure the fire was roarin' so it'd be warm for everybody else. Then she'd build the fire in her cook stove in the kitchen and put the coffee on. I could hear her singin' softly to herself, *"Amazing Grace, how sweet the sound, that saved a wretch like me. I once was lost but now I'm found. Was blind but now I see."* It was Mama's favorite. Mine, too.

Still sitting on the side of my bed and gazing out at the snow, I knew just exactly what she would do next. Even though we have electricity—and had for almost 5 years, Mama still enjoyed lighting the oil lamp on the table beside her rocking chair. She would sit down with her big Bible and read until the coffee was made and the house began to warm. Mama said that this was her "self-time". Time when she could do what she loved with out being interrupted by a child who needed her to do something—and time when she didn't feel pressed to do something that she knew was waiting her attention. She says that everybody needs some "self-time," and that if you look hard enough that you'll find it.

When the house begins to warm, she will come upstairs to each of her children, shake them gently and tell them to rise and shine and "Look at the day the Lord has made for us! Rejoice and be glad in it!" Then she'll go back down stairs, get Pa up and begin making breakfast. This happens every morning, just like clockwork. It never changes.

When she came upstairs this morning, and found me looking out the window, she sat down beside me for just a moment. "It's a winter wonderland, Lil' Jim. It's a winter wonderland." It sure was nice just to sit there snuggled up against her warm robe and watch the flakes fall. Mama always smells so good. Just like Granny Ruth's flower bed in the middle of summer.

"Where do you reckon they all come from, Mama? Think the clouds git all filled up until they can't hold no more and then the snow just kinda spills over the sides and falls down?" I asked as we gazed out the window. "Wonder if a cloud ever gets a big hole in it and they all fall out at once? Reckon that'd be like the blizzard that Daddy Robert always talks about back in '22? Boy, I sure would like to see it if that ever happened."

Mama just laughed, "You sure do have some imagination, Lil' Jim. Now get yourself on outta bed and come on down stairs where it's warm." She went to the others, before going downstairs and continuing her routine. "Git up, boys. Rise and Shine!" I can tell Mama likes the snow just as much as I do.

Everybody struggled to get out of their warm bed and hustle down the steps to get dressed by the stove. You could either stay upstairs and get dressed where it was so cold that you would have icicles hanging from your nose or you could go downstairs by the fire and dress with everybody else. It didn't take long to get over your embarrassment of havin' people see you in your underwear. "Mama, I c.c..can't find my...my...my other boot," Joe stammered as he struggled to pull the straps of his overalls over his warmest flannel shirt. "I k..k..know it was right h-h-here. Y.y..y..you seen it?"

"Look under the corner table, Joe, and stop all that yelling. I'm just right here. If you would hang your coat and stuff on your peg in the kitchen like you're suppose to, you'd be able to find things. Everybody make sure you dress warm. That snow's pretty, but it's real cold and I don't want nobody catchin' their death," Mama answered as she put the biscuits in the oven.

Nobody can eat until all the mornin' chores are done. Except Pa, that is. He always has to have his coffee—but I don't guess that's eatin'. He's already cleaned the snow off the back porch and steps as we're still puttin' on all the clothes we can find. Then he'll listen to the mornin' news and weather on the radio while he drinks his coffee before goin' out to the barn to make sure everything is ready for the day's work.

Queenie's box is still over in the corner of the porch. Still filled with the cedar shavins- like she'll be back in a minute. But she's been gone over six weeks and Pa's been all over the farm hollerin' and whistling for her. Hopin' she might show up somehow. We all take a look around the Hall place every time we pass but there ain't no sign of her there either. Reckon Pa's the only one that's holdin' out that she'll be found.

We have two cows. It's Maggie and Andy's job to milk. Maggie don't mind, but Andy hates it. Says it is girl's work—he should have a "man's job." But then he really don't like livin' on a farm. Says he is movin' to town and gettin a job where he don't have to work from daylight to dark just as soon as he graduates high school. Pa says he's dreamin.

Matt feeds the cows, the horse and Old Sam, the mule. He forks 'em some hay and this morning has to break the ice off the water trough so that they can get to it.

Betty feeds the chickens and gathers the eggs. She has them all named...there's Hilda, Francis, Hen Penny, Wilcie, Myrtle and Charlie, the rooster, and Gray Ghost, the goose. They follow her around the yard like she was their mama. And she talks to 'em all the time like they're her children. She never shuts up. Asks more questions than any school teacher. Reckon the chickens don't mind, though. They can't talk back.

Betty is all the time finding strays...dogs, cats, birds and such...that are sick or hurt. She brings them home, nurses them back to health and then tries to find a home for them. Mama says that every dog and cat in the county knows just where we live and that sometimes she doesn't think they are lost or sick at all. They just know where they can find a good meal. On her way home from school one day last fall, she found Gray Ghost on the riverbank stuck in the mud and washed up tree limbs. She worked for over a half-hour afore she finally got him free and came carryin' him to the house. Mama said she didn't know who was the worst off, Betty or that old goose; they were both covered from head to toe with dirt and mud.

Betty's afraid of the dark, especially at night when there's no one around. Thinks the boogieman's behind every tree just waitin' to jump out on her. But she's all right in the morning before the sun come up as long as she has her lantern and she can see the rest of us as we do our chores.

Me and Joe carry wood from the shed and fill the box on the back porch. We also fill the box in the kitchen next to the cook stove makin' sure there's plenty of kindling. In the winter time, especially when it's snowing, everybody moves a little faster cause it's mighty cold out there and you want to get back in close to the fire as soon as you can. It's kinda fun though 'cause the snow makes everythin' real quiet. All I can hear are our footsteps crunchin' as Joe and I make our trips from the woodshed to the house. "Hurry up, Joe! I could smell the fryin' bacon last trip," I called, loading my arms full of the frozen sticks for the last time. "My belly sounds like a big ole grizzly bear I'm so hungry."

"Radio says we're in for a good one," Pa announced when we all sat down at the table to Mama's hot biscuits, bacon and scrambled eggs. "Glad we got that extra wood chopped before Mort left."

Mama returned thanks before we dug in like we ain't eat in weeks. "You children won't have to go to school today and from the looks of it, probably not tomorrow. I still want you to do some extra homework, though. That way you won't be behind when you do go back," Mama said as she opened a big jar of honey. "A little extra reading and arithmetic never hurt anybody." Everybody groaned but knew that there ain't no use complainin'. If we don't get busy, the longer it's gonna be before we can git outside.

Everybody hurried with their chores and schoolwork. Nobody wanted to be left inside when everybody else was outside havin' so much fun. I put on two of everything…two pairs of socks, two pair of pants, and two shirts. I woulda put on two coats and two pair of gloves if I'd had 'em. I like the snow but I don't like to be cold!

"Hurry up, Joe! I see the Hall boys comin' up the road now," I called back as I stepped out on the front porch barely able to walk with all my clothes on. Hope I don't fall down, I might not be able to get back up. The snow was still falling, harder than ever. It was at least 6 inches deep, already. I believe the radio's right. "Hey, Lem! You and Hank wanna try out our new sled?" I hollered to the Hall brothers as they came through the gate. "Me and Joe'll race you down the hill!" Everybody was talking and laughing at the same time.

Hank and Lem are Johnny Lee Hall's younger brothers. Hank's in my grade at school but he don't come all the time. Says his Pa needs him at home. I heard our teacher, Miz Frady, tell him one time that he shouldn't miss so much that he was gonna get left behind. Said she was gonna have a talk with his Ma and Pa about his attendance. Hank just hung his head and said that there weren't no need that he try to come more. But he ain't been there hardly a'tall this winter and I ain't had the chance to ask him about Queenie. Maybe I can catch him beside hisself and see what I can find out today. "Hey, Hank, you think you got enough clothes on? You look like some big, wooly bear. How many coats you got on?"

"As many as I could find. I'd a put on more if I'd had 'em!" Hank called back as he pulled his sled through the gate. The Hall boys have a sled, too, but it ain't like our Flexible Flyer. If you rub candle wax on the runners, it'll go real fast but I'll bet it won't go as fast as ours.

Betty, Matt and Maggie were already in the yard. Andy went to the can house to get our sled. Matt had found a candle and put it in his pocket. Before long, at least 20 kids, big ones and little ones, had gathered in our pasture at the foot of "Giant Hill" to ride what ever they could find. Sheepback Mountain may not be worth too much when it comes to farmin' but everybody knows it's the best sleddin in these parts. Kids just kept coming up our road, bundled up in everything they could get on. Some pulled real sleds, some had old inner tubes or pieces of metal—one even had an old meat tray from the packing plant to ride on. Pa built a fire over to one side at the bottom so we could gather around to get warm before goin' to the top and comin' down again.

"Hey Matt," I whispered, pointing at the latest three arrivals. "Ain't that the colored boy that the Sheriff was talkin' about? Over there with Billy and Sam."

"Yeah, looks like it. Wonder what he's doin' here?" Matt answered starring after the three as they pulled their sled up the hill. "Hey, Andy! Look over there."

"Yeah, I saw him. Told him to come on over and warm by the fire but he just kinda keeps to himself," Andy told his brother, handing the sled to Betty. "Looks to me like he just wants to ride like the rest of us."

Nobody seemed to pay any attention to the stranger. He rode a few times. Always with the two boys he came with, not saying a word. You could hardly tell he was different from anyone else with all the clothes on.

Seems Maggie and Johnny Lee Hall spend a lot of time warmin' by the fire and not sledin'. But that's OK 'cause that means we can ride more and don't have to take turns as much.

"Hey, Johnny Lee, we ain't never found Queenie. You know anything about her?" Andy asked as Johnny Lee stepped in close to the fire after a trip down the hill.

"No! I done told you afore. I don't know nothing about no missing dog. Why would I know anything?"

"Well, your Pa sure did want one of her pups so I figure that he mighta took her so he could have 'em all. She'd had 'em and by now and they'd be old enough to sell or maybe give to them Klan fellers. Your Pa been wearin' a white robe and mask and goin' round burnin' crosses?" Andy accused.

"He wanted one alright. Had the money to buy it, too. But he didn't steal it. How many times I gotta tell you, Andy! My Pa ain't no thief. And I don't know what you're talking about. Ain't no Klan around here."

"You two quit arguing. Andy, you ought to know that Johnny Lee don't know anything about Queenie. Now,

I've heard enough. Come on Johnny Lee, ride down with me," Maggie urged.

"Don't know nothing about your Pa's dog, Maggie. Honest," he said as they sat on the sled.

"Oh, never mind Andy, Johnny Lee. You know he's always been a hot head. Shoots his mouth off before he thinks. Just forget about it and let's have some fun!" Away they went, but the accusation was not forgotten.

"Come on Hank we gotta git on home. Lem get our sled." Johnny Lee called to his brothers as everyone else started moving toward the house thinking of the hot chocolate Mama had promised everyone.

"Don't go, Johnny Lee. Mama's gonna make hot chocolate for all of us. Come on over to the house for a few minutes and get warm," Maggie urged as she tugged at his sleeve. "Andy won't say nothin in front of Pa about Queenie, I promise. Come on and git some chocolate."

"Come on, Johnny Lee, let's just git one cup. We'll hurry and drink it and be gone afore you know it. Just a couple of more minutes," Hank and Lem both begged their older brother.

"We gotta git, now, boys. Pa's gonna be real mad if he gits home and we're not there. He's been gone off for two days and it ain't like him to be gone this long, not in this weather. Maybe we can sneak off tomorrow and ride some more. This stuff ain't gonna melt for a long time. Come on Lem, you and Hank, come on now. I ain't gonna wait no longer. Maggie, tell, your pa 'thank ye' for letting us ride and for buildin' the fire. And tell him that I don't know nothing about Queenie. If I did, I tell 'em, I swear," he called back as he started through the pasture with the younger boys slowly, reluctantly, trailing after him.

"Y'all come back tomorrow!" She called after them as she pulled her scarf tight.

"Hey! What's your name? Mine's Betty. I ain't never seen you afore. You comin' in for hot chocolate?" Betty put her hand on the stranger's arm trying to keep him from leaving. "You live around here? You don't go to our school. You quit like my brother Mort?"

The stranger stopped, looked down at the muddy snow, and just shook his head.

"Cat got your tongue? What's the matter? Don't you talk?" Betty kept on with her endless questions.

"Name's Nathaniel," he finally answered. "I'm livin' with my folks. Don't go to school here. Gotta go. Pleased to meet you, Betty," he answered as he pulled his arm away, trying not to be impolite. He almost ran down the road.

"Come back tomorrow, you hear. And stay for cocoa next time!" Betty yelled after him as she turned and headed toward Maggie and me. "You all know that feller? I ain't never seen him afore. Seems a little different don't he?"

"No, I don't know him. But I know that he is Ned and Susie Putnam's boy. And I'm not sure Mama would like it if you invite him in for cocoa, Betty," Maggie answered, not sure what she should say to her younger sister.

"Why, Mama says you gotta be nice to everybody. Different or not. Why do you reckon he don't go to school? Why ain't I ever seen him before?" Betty questioned no one in particular as she sloshed through the snow toward the house. "He sure don't talk much."

"Come on Maggie, let's git to the house afore the cocoa's all gone," I told her as we watched the Hall boys make a trail through the fresh snow. Nathanial, a few steps behind and with his head hung low, made his way toward town. "Boy, I sure am glad that our Pa ain't like that, ain't you? I think those boys have a real hard time, and their Ma, too."

"Yeah, I do. But I wish hothead Andy would keep his mouth shut. There's no way that Johnny Lee knows anything about Queenie. And Andy accusing him like that just makes him feel real bad," she answered taking my hand. "Let's get inside, all of a sudden I'm real cold."

CHAPTER 4

IN-DOOR PLUMBIN'

I'M NOT REAL CERTAIN when our house was built but I know it was a long time ago. We've got a downstairs and an upstairs and a big front porch and a little back porch. The kids all sleep upstairs in two big rooms except for Brother Mort, afore he left. His bed was downstairs in one corner of the sittin' room. Said he was too grown to sleep upstairs with children. Mama and Pa's bedroom is just off the sittin' room. There's a big kitchen with a long table where we can all gather around. That's where we usually sit on Saturday night and listen to the Grand Ole Opry on Pa's radio. Matt likes Flat and Scruggs—that's Lester Flat and Earl Scruggs. They play blue grass and Matt tries to play along with 'em on his guitar. Mama says that he's gettin' pretty good but I think that she just tells him that.

We've got a woodshed not far from the back door and the springhouse, can house and chicken coop are just over from that. The big barn is down in the field some. The only other building we got is the outhouse and it moves around.

Every spring, Pa picks a spot and Mort, before he left to join up, and Andy dig a hole. Pa hitches the mule up to the sled and Mort, Matt and Joe help him lay the outhouse over on it. Then we all stand on the sides of the sled to keep it from fallin' off and pull the outhouse to the new hole and stand it up again. Mort and Andy throw some lime in the old hole and fill 'er up with dirt.

It's a big deal ever spring just where the new outhouse needs to be. Mama wants it real close cause, ya' see, she don't like snakes. One time, long about dark, she was kinda in a hurry to get to the outhouse when she just about stepped on a big old copperhead that was stretched out across the trail. She started screamin' and jumpin' up and down and runnin' back to the house. Pa came a runnin' with the hoe and kilt that snake but it was too late for Mama. She didn't need to go to the outhouse then. Next mornin', she made Pa move it closer to the house and it wasn't even spring.

We have just about run outta places close to the house to put it. You can't put it near the spring or the well and you sure don't want it in the front yard. I heard Mama and Pa talking about it long after I went to bed. "R.L. it's time. We've put it off long enough. Maggie's gettin of age when she needs her privacy and there's just not another place to put the outhouse this year."

"Now, Vadie, we're farm folk not town folk. We don't need no high-falutin things. Why, we got electricity, next thing I know, you'll be wantin' a dad-burn telephone." They kept on talkin but real low so nobody could hear and I finally went to sleep.

Next morning was Saturday and right after breakfast, Pa had Andy and Matt and Joe all out beside the kitchen diggin a big hole. I thought, "Boy, this sure is gonna be some outhouse cause that's one big hole and it ain't ever been this close to the house, either."

"Lil' Jim, come with me, we're goin to town," Pa called as he got in his truck. He was actin' kinda mad so I didn't know if I really wanted to go with him or not. But I got in and we rode on to town with nobody sayin' nothing. "Lil' Jim, go into Daddy Robert's store and get us some 10 penny nails. I'm goin on down to the lumberyard and I'll pick you up on my way back."

My Grandpa Crawford (that's Pa's Pa), everybody calls him "Daddy Robert," has the store in town. It's right down next to the railroad track and he sells everything. Mama Annie Crawford works in the store sometimes when they are busy, usually around payday at the plant. I like to go by there after school sometimes when I don't have chores waitin' for me at home. There's all kinds of nails and screws to build 'bout anything. He even has seeds for plantin a garden and rakes, hoes and shovels. Then, over on one side, he has some canned groceries, flour, and corn meal and stuff like that. Daddy Robert likes to brag, "If you can't find it at Crawford's Store, then you just don't need it." Folks go over to the county seat to get most of their groceries but they git about everything else here.

Mama Annie is the best cook in these parts, just ask anybody and she's always got pies and cakes and cookies for sale. There's always a big pot of coffee on the potbelly stove that stands in the middle of the store and it's free for anybody that wants a cup.

On Saturday mornings, there's a group of men who sit in chairs on the porch of the store when the weather's warm. Everybody calls them the "Sit and Spit" club 'cause that's what they do. They just sit there talkin' about the weather or crops or politics or such while they chew their tobacco and spit in some old tin cans that Daddy Robert keeps handy. Some of 'em don't have too gooda aim and miss from time to time, so you have to watch where your stepin'. Sometimes they gather up even if ain't Saturday. When the weather turns cold, they come inside and sit by the stove. Guess they must be important men 'cause Daddy Robert says "They're solving the world's problems," whenever I ask him about 'em. Daddy Robert and Mama Annie live in a little house just next door to the store and if

I'm not at the store, then I like to be there cause it always smells so good. The railroad track runs right behind the store and their house. Sometimes, when I get to stay the night, I like to stay awake and listen for the train. It's whistle sounds like it's sayin' "Come on...come on...." I like to pretend that I'm on it and am goin' to some far away place.

There's a bank and a few other stores in town, too, where you can get clothes and furniture and stuff. We ain't got a stop light like they have over in Waynesville, the county seat. Guess when there just one road right through the middle of town, you don't need a stop light.

I was always glad to go to Daddy Robert's store. Maybe Mama Annie would be in there and give me one of her cookies.

"Mornin, Lil' Jim. What brings you to town so early this morning?" Daddy Robert asked as he sat on the porch drinkin' coffee and talkin' to old man Mears of the Sit and Spit Club. A few of the other members were just straggling up to take their places.

"Pa dropped me off to get some 10 penny nails while he went on down to the lumberyard," I quickly answered looking around for Mama Annie and her cookies. Mr. Mears just grinned, letting tobacco juice leak out of both corners of his mouth before he wiped it off with his shirtsleeve. I heard him say once that if a man was real level-headed the 'backie would come out of both sides of his mouth but I think he was just joshin'.

"Mornin' Bob," Mr. Mears called as Bob Thompson pulled his chair across the board porch so he could lean it against the store. Seems that everybody had just their spot, their assigned chair, and knew just where they were suppose to be in order to observe and make comments about the goin and comin at Crawford's Store and most of the other stores in town for that matter.

"Nails. Now just what would you all be needin with nails?" But Daddy Robert already had gone inside and got a small brown paper bag and was fillin' it up.

Following him inside, "I don't know. I think we must be moving the outhouse. Andy, Matt and Joe are at the house diggin a hole next to the kitchen and you outta see it, Daddy Robert. It's a big 'un. We must be gonna have some kinda outhouse," I answered just as Mama Annie came in the back door with a plate of hot cookies.

"Lil' Jim, you must have a nose like a blood hound if you could smell these cookies all the way to your house," She said as she smiled and stuck the plate out in front of me.

"He done come in with his Pa for some nails and R.L.'s gone down to the lumberyard," Daddy Robert answered before I could say a word. "They're movin' their outhouse next to the kitchen."

"Yeah, and Andy, Matt and Joe are diggin a great big hole, Mama Annie. Biggest hole you've ever saw," I added as I took one of the warm peanut butter cookies from the plate. They were my favorite.

"I'll just bet she's finally talked him into it," Mama Annie leaned over and whispered in Daddy Robert's ear but loud enough for me to hear. "And it's about time, too," she told him before turning to me. "Lil' Jim, Hank Simmons, the Postmaster, said your Mama got another letter from Mort this week. What'd it say? He doin' all right?"

"Reckon so. Said Army life was hard and all but that he was glad he joined up. Food's not as good as Mama's but there's plenty of it. Says there's a lot of talk about maybe havin' to go off and fight in someplace called Korea. He don't know if he'll have to go or not. Mama don't talk much about it. Just folds the letter back up and sticks it in the back of her BIBLE with the rest," I answered hopin' she'd tell me who had talked who into what and maybe give me another one of them good smellin' cookies.

Other customers drifted into the store then and I nibbled slowly on my cookie tryin' to make it last until Pa got back. Ned Putnam and his boy, Nathaniel, kinda eased in past the members of the club. Bought some flour and other stuff before the older man tipped his hat to Mama Annie, "Nice to see you, Miz Crawford. Hope you're well."

"Doin' fine, Ned. Hope you are. Nathaniel, glad you're back in town. Hope you're planning on staying awhile."

"Yes, Ma'ma," was all that he answered before tipping his hat and following his father toward the front of the store. Daddy Robert stopped Mr. Putnam just as he started to open the door. "Ned, heard about what happened. Want you to know you and your family are welcome here anytime. You're good folk and ain't no need for anybody to go to actin' like that. You come to me if there's anything I can do to help."

Daddy Robert stuck out his hand. Mr. Putnam finally took it and they shook. All the old colored man could do was shake his head as he left the store.

"That Nathaniel has grown into a fine looking young man," Mama Annie commented to her husband when he came back to the cash register. "Stands tall. Wonder how old he is?"

"Pa said he was near Andy's age," I told her, wanting to sound grown-up. "He came sleigh ridin' back in February. Sheriff said some fellers done burned a cross in their yard."

"Really," she said, looking at her husband with a questioning look. "Robert, what do you know about that?"

"Not now, Annie," he answered. "Not in front of the boy. We'll talk about it later," and walked back toward the front of the store just as Mrs. Trull came in. "Good morning, Sarah. What can we do for you this morning?"

Daddy Robert let me help Mrs. Trull take her groceries out to her car and she gave me a nickel. Said I was good help. The group of men on the porch grew until there were at least 10 or 12, drinkin their coffee and puttin' in their first chew of the morning.

Mr. Hall came in. He was by himself. Don't reckon he's a member of the club 'cause he didn't even slow down as he stepped in and shoved the door back. None of the men on the porch spoke to him either. He went to the back of the store. Talked to Daddy Robert real quite and then left without buyin nothing. Guess Mrs. Hall don't need nothing this morning. Wish I coulda asked him if Hank was sick or something 'cause he ain't been to school in a spell. But I was scared cause he was lookin' real mad. He always wears the same floppy, brown felt hat pulled down so you really can't see his eyes. And he never seems to smile, or so as you would notice. Don't know that I ever heard him say anything nice, or excuse me or nothin'. Sure am glad my Pa's my Pa. Even on days like today when he's kinda grumpy.

It wasn't long until I saw Pa pull the truck up in front of the store. It was loaded down with lumber. All kinds and all sizes. It was sticking out the back and dragging the ground. I never saw so much lumber except at the mill. "You got the nails?" He yelled out the truck window as I stood on the sidewalk starin at the truck along with the Sit 'n Spit fellers.

"Yes, sir!" I said, showing him the bag and runnin' around to the other side to climb in.

Daddy Robert and Mama Annie came to the door of the store and looked at Pa's load. "Aren't you coming in, R.L.?" Mama Annie asked.

"Gotta get on home. Gotta lot of work to do," he grumbled.

Mama Annie just could not control herself, "Don't mean to be nosy, R.L., but what are you doin with all that lumber?"

"Buildin' an in-door bathroom!" he answered a little short. "Don't know why the outhouse ain't good enough no more."

Mama Annie and Daddy Robert just stood there on the porch and smiled. All the club members just smiled, too, and nodded their heads as we drove off. They were all still smillin' as we drove outta sight.

On the way home, I got my courage up to ask Pa about David Lee Hall. "Pa, Mr. Hall come in the store but didn't buy nothin."

"That right?" he asked as we drove toward home.

"Yeah," I answered trying to figure out how to ask. "I wanted to ask him if Hank was sick or something cause he ain't been in school, but he looked real mad. Why do you reckon he's like that all the time?"

"Guess he thinks he's been dealt a short hand, Lil' Jim. Some folk just don't appreciate the blessins the Lord has given to 'em," he answered as he patted my knee.

"Well, he sure is scary, with his hat pulled down so you can't look him in the eye. And I think Lem and Hank are scared of him, too, and Johnny Lee. Daddy Robert says you can't trust a man that don't look ye in the eye."

"Well, I don't think you have anything to be afraid of. Most of the time people like him are all bark and no bite."

"Pa, Andy's real certain that he knows something about Quennie. Do you think he took her?"

"Don't know 'Lil Jim. Ain't never seen no pups around his house and I always look real close when we pass. But he shore did want one real bad that day he was at the house. But ye just can't go accusing somebody without proof. Like I said afore, sometimes people do a lot of talkin and their mouth gets 'em in trouble."

"Mr. Putnam and his boy came in, too. They didn't say much. Looked kinda scared to me."

"Well, Lil' Jim, guess they don't know just who they can trust. Don't know who might have been hidin' behind those white robes and masks and what they might do next. When you're the only colored folks livin' round here and a group of fellers start givin' you a hard time, probably would make you a little bit nervous," his Pa tried to explain. "But my guess is that all that Klan business is over and done with. They've had their say and have moved on to some other place where they can stir up trouble. Ain't nothing' for you to worry your head about."

We didn't talk the rest of the way. Guess we was both thinkin'. Nathaniel Putnam seemed like a nice enough feller. Looked to be about Andy's age, maybe a little older. Don't know why anybody would care if he said "howdy" to a girl—white or not. I figure that's just the polite thing to do. And I sure don't know what blessin' the Lord's done give to me but I decided right then and there that I would tell Him "thank ye" every night until I had it figured out. I ain't never gonna not look people in the eye either or let my mouth git me in trouble.

The Putnam car was silent, too. Ned and his son were both wrapped up in their thoughts. Hazelgrove was about the only home Ned had ever known. He and his Susie had move here almost 40 years ago from Waynesville. They moved into the little blue house just across the tracks from the mill where Ned had gotten a job as janitor. Susie helped Mrs. Miller and Mrs. Sheppard with their cooking, laundry, babies and such. Between the two of them, there was enough to get by on—especially when their vegetable garden was plentiful.

The doctor over in Waynesville told Susie right off that she wouldn't have no babies of her own, so they took comfort in each other. Then, low and behold, just like Sarah in the Bible, she got pregnant and Nathaniel was born. Life was good.

By the time Nathaniel was six, it became clear that they would have to send him somewhere else. He was always on the outside looking in. Oh, the other parents and children were friendly enough—they would "howdy" and pat his head saying things like, "Boy, Ned, that boy's gonna' be taller than you one of these days." But that is as far as it ever went. He never had a friend. And school was out of the question, unless they sent him on the almost hour ride to Waynesville every day so he could be with his own. So the decision was made, they would let him live in Charlotte with Susie's mother where there would be lots of friends and a school close-by. Nathaniel would come back from time to time—holidays, summer vacations and such but it became very clear that he soon thought of Charlotte as "home." The visits to Ned and Susie's became fewer and fewer as he became a teenager.

Sheriff Taylor had stopped by several times in the past few weeks—ever since the "incident", as he called it. He had no idea of who might have been behind the masks or even if they were from Hazelgrove. But he sure didn't want Klan trouble to start brewing, no matter where they might be comin' from. So the Sheriff suggested that the whole family move, maybe to Waynesville or even better somewhere that no one knew them or anything about what had happened. But Ned was dead set against it. "We're stayin'," he told the Sheriff. "Ain't nobody gonna' run us off. We ain't done nothing. Nathaniel's a good boy. He'll stay close to home until this all blows over." But he sounded a lot more sure than he was. The cotton on the top of his head and under his chin had gotten a little whiter in the past few weeks. Even though it was just a little piece and she had done it for years, Susie was afraid to walk home from the Millers and Sheppards by herself—so he went by and picked her up each evening. The men at the plant seemed a little stand-offish. They still said "howdy" and all, but that was as far as it went. Never the laughing, kidding, and slap on the back as it once was.

Nathaniel was very withdrawn. He never ventured out. He sat on his bed and read the few books he had brought with him. Today's trip to town was his first. And with the whispers and strange looks, it might just be his last.

Ned had never been a quitter, but maybe they should take the Sheriff's advice.

BY THE NEXT SATURDAY, we had the toilet and tub set up in the little room and water run from the well. There would be no more carrying water to fill the big tub in the kitchen for baths. We could just put the stopper in the bottom of the bathtub, turn on the water and fill 'er up. Course, you still had to heat water on the stove and pour it in if you wanted a warm bath. This just might not be too bad after all if you didn't have to do it more than once a week. And what with it so easy to fill up and let out, maybe I could take a bath in fresh water once in a while, not water that Joe and Betty had already took a bath in.

Mama hung a quilt over the doorway so nobody could peak in. She also hummed a lot after that when she was workin' in the kitchen and ever once in a while I'd see her go over and just look in the new bathroom and smile. I think Pa was really proud of the new in-door bathroom, too. I heard him tell Mama one day, "Now Vadie, this is it. No more new fangled contraptions. No more, Vadie, now you hear!"

Mama just smiled and said, "Yes, Dear." I never heard my Mama call Pa anything but R.L. before that.

CHAPTER 5

THE RAMP CONVENTION

EVERY YEAR IN THE EARLY SPRING when the dogwoods start to bloom and everything's turning green, my Mama sends all the kids up on the mountain to hunt ramps. Now if you've never dug any ramps, or ate any ramps, then it's hard to understand just what they mean to us mountain folk. You see, they grow wild in a cove up on the mountain. They kinda look like little green onions only they have wider leaves. But what's so different about 'em is how they smell—or how they make you smell. You see, anybody that eats ramps smells bad, at least for a couple of days. But if you eat 'em raw, they make you smell real bad for a long, long time. My Granny Ruth says they smell worse than any skunk. She's the only one in Hazelgrove, that I know, that don't like ramps.

"I only eat 'em out of self-defense. Can you just imagine what it would be like to be the only one around town who doesn't eat ramps!" She's quick to say.

Pa says that folks around here been eatin ramps since the first white folks moved in, about 200 years ago. Some people claim that they will cure what ails you. Now I ain't so sure about that but I do know that Mama usually fixes two or three messes every spring and me and my brothers and sisters ain't hardly ever sick; except for bug bites, stumped toes, and such. But then I've never heard nobody say that ramps was good for that.

There's a Ramp Festival held over next to the river every spring. Folks from all around come right after church the last Sunday in April.

The Crawfords are all members of the Shady Hill Baptist Church. It's in town. We got a Methodist church in town, too, but I don't know too many people who go there. It's the First Methodist Church. Don't know if there's a Second Methodist Church anywhere or not. Pa says it's mostly rich folk who are Methodist or folks who'd like to think they got more 'n most. It's not as big as the Baptist Church, so I guess we ain't got too many rich people around here. My Grandpa Caldwell (that's Mama's daddy) was the preacher at Shady Hill until he passed away 'bout two years back. Now we got Rev. Thomas and his wife, Miz Pearl. My Granny Ruth Caldwell says it's just not the same without Grandpa up there in the pulpit. Says Rev. Thomas is just too young and wet behind the ears to know about what the Lord expects of us. Don't preach enough hell fire and damnation, she says. I think he does. Shucks, one Sunday, he hit the pulpit so hard with his fist that a corner of the wood broke off and went flying through the air. It almost hit Miss Grace Lowe, our organ player, right on the side of her head. Don't nobody doze off to sleep any more at Shady Hill. Granny Ruth still goes on Sundays, and sits in her same pew but leaves through the back door so she won't have to shake the preacher's hand. Guess she's heard enough sermons to know what the Lord expects.

As soon as church is over everybody shows up at the river. The ladies spread checkered cloths on the picnic tables and bring out their best recipes. There's always lots of fried chicken and potato salad and Mama Annie's chocolate pies and the other regular picnic stuff. But what everybody comes for are the ramps! They can be fixed lots of ways, put in beans, or taters, or salad, or chopped up and mixed with scrambled eggs. All the ladies take great pride in their ramp recipes and try to come up with a new one every year.

Me and Joe like 'em best in eggs if we have to eat 'em cooked. I really like 'em raw. It's not that I really like to eat 'em raw but that's the way they make you smell the worst for the longest. Nobody seems to notice that you smell bad at the festival, though, cause everybody's eatin' 'em, even Granny Ruth. So everybody smells the same.

Mr. Riley, the principal at Hazelgrove Grammar School, just goes ahead and announces that school will be closed for two days every year following the ramp festival. He knows that when you have a room full of ramp smellin' kids that there won't be much learnin done. Mama won't let me and Joe eat 'em raw cause she knows we won't be able to go back to school for a lot more days.

If you eat ramps and come to school smellin' bad, they make you sit out in the hall. Sometimes there are more kids in the hall than in the rooms. And it sure don't do much good to have 'em sit in the hall, cause soon, the whole building begins to smell and you have to raise up all the windows. And you sure don't want to be the only one who's not eat any cause you'd probably pass out or something.

My friend, Harvey Brown, said his brother told him about the time in real early spring when the ramps first started peakin up outta the ground, somebody snuck, chopped 'a bunch of 'em up real fine and put 'em in a pot of taters that was cookin on the stove in the school cafeteria. At first, nobody could figure out what the smell was or where it was coming from until some of the kids started eatin. They had to close school for 3 days to get the smell out. Harvey's brother said everybody knew that it was Andy that put the ramps in that pot and somebody told Mr. Riley and he made Andy work after school for two weeks scrubbin the kitchen.

All the folks from Shady Hill Baptist drove up about the same time. The folks from First Methodist were already there and their ladies already had most of the tables covered. The Methodists don't hold as long on Sunday as us Baptist. I reckon they don't have as many sins to repent of.

I helped Mama get our stuff out of the truck and carry it over to the first available table. All the lady folk started helpin' Mama empty her basket. They was making a fuss over her good smellin' dishes and askin' when she had heard from Mort and if he liked the army. "I only have had three letters to amount to anything. Mort was never one to write. Says he'll be finished with basic training and will be home in three weeks on leave. Reckon that'll help R.L. get his tobacco out. Just wish he hadn't gone and done something so foolish," I heard her tell 'em as she suddenly became very busy tryin to find a spot to store her basket. I ran on off to find Harvey. He was probably already throwin rocks in the river by now.

All the men were gathered around over next to the Henry Wiggin's truck talkin' about how long they'd had their tobacco beds sowed. I stopped by on my way to the river to listen for a minute.

Henry said he'd put his in early March 'cause he was sure we were going to have a warm spring. "The wooly worms were real black last fall and the shucks on the corn were real thick. That's a sure sign we were in for a long, cold winter and this was one of the hardest ones we've had in a spell. Wasn't much snow; just that late one in February but it sure was cold and wet," Henry told the men as they all nodded their heads in agreement. "A warm spring always follows a hard winter." All the men listened real careful 'cause Henry always knows all about weather and signs and his crops were always the best of anybody's in these parts. "I'm settin' my tobacco in the ground come the first. Already got my plowin' done," he said. "I'm not waitin' until after the 10th 'cause the signs won't be right. Gotta plant when the moon's increasing to have a good crop."

They all nodded again secretly hoping that Henry was right 'cause a late frost would destroy their crop and they wouldn't be able to feed their families through the next winter. You could bet that every farm would have their tobacco off the bed and in the ground before May 10th. That is exceptin' for David Lee Hall. He don't believe in plantin' tobacco. Says it's too much work. "I got me better ways of spendin' my time and got a lot more dollars to show for it, too," he told the group. Most of the men just went on talkin' and paid him no mind. Don't know what he plants but maybe Pa could ask him so we wouldn't have to work so hard, I thought as I ran on to find Harvey.

Just as the ladies were about to finish getting everything put out on the tables, around the bend came a whole string of fancy cars. They were all long and black and shinned up real nice. Not a farm truck among 'em. When they stopped, out came a whole passel of men dressed in Sunday-go-to-meetin clothes like I ain't never seen. Why, one was a big fat man with a white suit and white shoes. They began to make their way toward the tables and tippin' their hats to all the ladies. They'd say things like, "My, you sure do look nice today, must be a new hat," and "I just know you got the best fried chicken in these mountains," and shook all their hands as they moved from table to table. Then they came over to where the men folk were gathered.

I scrambled up next to Daddy Robert and was just about to ask him who in the world all those fancy people were when the big man in the white suit comes up to him and tries to shake his hand. But Daddy Robert just put his hand in his pocket. "How's the store goin, Robert? This can't be R.L.'s boy, he's gettin tall as a tree. Hope I can count on your vote in November and Miss Annie's, too." Then he bent down, rubbed my head and shook my hand before movin' on to the next man. Every one of 'em came by. Sometimes Daddy Robert shook their hand and they'd say nice things and how they was countin on Daddy Robert's support. But sometimes Daddy Robert would just put his hand in his pocket.

Everybody began to separate into two groups. One group stood over near the big Oak tree and began to talk to the crowd...like preachin' or something. The big fat man in the white suit took his group and climbed up in the back of Mr. Foster's truck. He began talking real loud and a small group of the town folk went over to listen. They were mostly from the Methodist Church. Me and Daddy Robert went over to listen to the man who was talking under the Oak tree. Pretty soon Mama and Pa, Mr. and Mrs. Hall and some other folks were gathered around to find out what he had to say.

Neither group stayed very long. They had their say, shook some more hands, then got in their fancy cars and left. They didn't eat nothin'. Reckon they must not like ramps. After they left, I asked Daddy Robert who they were. "They're politicians, boy. Old Bob Bennett's runnin' for congress and Sam McGuire's runnin' for the senate."

"How about the man in the white suit? What's he runnin for?" I asked.

"He's a Republican, Lil' Jim. We don't vote for no Republicans. They're just out for the rich folks and for makin' their self rich. All us Crawfords are Yellow Dog Democrats! and proud of it. We don't cotton to no Republicans," he answered spitting tobacco juice on the ground. About that time, someone called out lunch was ready and we made our way over to the tables.

It sure was confusin'. I didn't know I was a "Yellow Dog", why I don't even know what that means; and I sure don't know what a Republican is. Shucks, the Republican in the white suit shook my hand and rubbed my head. How am I supposed to know the difference? He looked just like the rest of them fellers. I'll have to ask Pa, he'll know. Bet this will give the Sit and Spit Club plenty to talk about next Saturday.

"You ever hear anything about your dog, R.L.?" Henry Wiggins ask Pa as we filled our plates.

"Nope," was all Pa could answer. It was still a sore subject.

"Well, I heard that some feller over 'bout Hendersonville had some nice pups for sale about the end of February. Wouldn't that been about the time your litter woulda been ready?" he continued as he piled the potato salad on his plate.

"Reckon so. But I don't hold no hope for figuring it out. Don't know how you'd go about provin' that a pup was yourn, anyway. But I sure would like to have Queenie back. She's a good dog," Pa answered. "Lil' Jim, make sure you get some vegetables. Don't just fill up on that chicken."

"Well, you ought to mosey on over there and check it out anyway. Can't never tell what you might find," Henry continued. He didn't want to let it drop. "Wouldn't surprise me none if David Lee didn't have something to do with it, either. Don't trust that one. Don't know many people who do. Maybe we ought to just git us a bunch of men together and take a look around his place."

"No, we can't go doin nothing like that. It'd just stir up more trouble. What goes around, comes around. If he did have a hand in it, it'll come out sooner or later," Pa answered. "Come on Lil' Jim, bring your plate and go over and sit with your Ma."

"What do you think about this Klan business? Don't reckon they've been back," he kept on talkin'.

"Ain't heard no more about it. Ned and Susie Putnam don't deserve that kind of trouble. They're good folk. Mind their own business and work hard. Don't think any Hazelgrove men were involved. At least, I sure hope not," Pa finished and walked away, not wanting to talk about it.

After lunch was over, and everybody's belly was full of all the good stuff that was brought, Sam Harkins and his boys went over to their truck and got out their banjo and guitars. Luke Green brought out his fiddle and even Matt had brought his guitar. I knew right then and there we were fixin to have us some good music. Better than the Grand Ole Opry on the radio on Saturday nights. I wonder if Mr. Harkins and Luke Green are Yellow Dogs like me and Daddy Robert?

MR. AND MRS. HALL and their three boys were among the first to leave. "Hazel, get our stuff together. We gotta get on home," David Lee ordered, even before the music had hardly begun. "Hank, go find your brothers! We got work to do. Can't be sittin' around here all afternoon lollygagging'!" he ordered as his youngest son ran by with a group of other boys. "Johnny Lee's probably over there under that tree with half the other boys in town tryin' to sassy up to that Crawford girl. Tell him to get hisself to the truck. And he'd better be quick about it," he continued to bark, not caring who heard.

Hazel Hall did as she was told. She gathered the few leftovers from today's lunch and placed them in her picnic basket. "Wish you all didn't have to leave so early, Hazel. The fun's just gettin' started," several of the ladies told her as they helped her gather her things and try to ease the embarrassment.

"That shore was good potato salad you brought. Don't know anybody that makes it any better," Vadie offered.

"Thank ye for your help. Guess David Lee's got chores for us. It was a nice afternoon, though," she answered with her head bowed, trying not to let anyone see the tears. She made her way toward their truck clutching the almost empty basket, just as David Lee and the boys got there.

"Here, Mama, I'll hold the basket back here," Johnny Lee told her as he took the now not so heavy load from her and climbed into the back of their old, broken down truck. "Sure do hope that there's some of your potato salad left," he commented, trying to divert his father's attention and ease the tension.

"There'd better be! Hazel brought enough to feed the whole county. Don't know why you have to bring so much!" He scolded her, not caring who heard. "All these uppity folk think they're better 'n us. Look down their nose, they do. Well, we don't have to sit around here all afternoon listenin' to their braggin'. Get in, we're goin'," he announced to his family as several people looked on and shook their heads.

He wasn't always like this, Hazel thought trying to remember the way it used to be. It had really gotten worse only in the last couple of years. Seems like it really started when he built that still up on the mountain behind their house. Back in '42 when the war had just begun, Johnny Lee was 9, Lem 5, and Hank was a babe in arms. David Lee had proudly announced that he was going to volunteer. She hadn't wanted him to go. Not and leave her with three small children and no way to feed them. But he had insisted. "It's every man's duty to sign up. Sides that, I'll be sending you money regular," he had assured her. "The Army pays its men real good."

He was gone for a little over a year and a half and she only had four penny postcards in all that time. Each with only a few words scrawled on them 'cause David Lee could barely read or write. Never any money or an address where she could write him back. She knew from some other men who had returned on leave after basic training that the Army had rejected David Lee because he was deaf in his right ear. "Huntin' accident," he had told her when they were first married. "My big brother shot a gun too close to my ear and I ain't been able to hear good since."

When he finally did show back up that day, Hazel almost didn't recognize him. He was much thinner and walked with a limp. "Got shot guardin' them slant-eyed Japs. Shoulda shot 'em all. They ain't good for nothin' except sneakin' around. Army sent me packin'. Said I weren't no good with this here limp," he lied when she ask him about how he had gotten hurt.

But Hazel knew that this was not true. Another Hazelgrove soldier on leave had seen him drunk and in a bar fight where he had gotten his leg cut with a broken bottle. When the soldier had returned home, he had innocently asked her how David Lee was doing.

She didn't tell David Lee she knew the truth, that he'd never been in the army…hadn't been hurt in the line of duty. She just let him ramble on about the war and the government and how that they didn't take care of their own. What could his stories possibly hurt? She wanted to keep his pride intact.

But as the years went by, the war tales grew taller and the anger got worse. He would sit her and the children down almost every night and make them listen as he rambled on for hours. Sometimes he slurred his words so bad in his drunken state that it was difficult to understand what he was saying. At first, Lem and Hank didn't understand. Johnny Lee was old enough and at first believed but then began to doubt as the stories got wilder. Sometimes he would sneak and ask his mother but she always would just say, "That's what your Pa says, Johnny. Who are we to question?"

David Lee's drinking became worse, too. When he decided to build the still, it seems that everything began to crumble. He would drink, shove her around and maybe even black her eye if something was not done just to his liking. He would lock the boys in their room, sometimes for days and tell them if he heard even a squeak out of them he would take the razor strap to their hides.

Hazel was ashamed. And afraid. He was her husband, father of her children. There was nothing she could do. She still tried to take the boys to church on Sundays, if she didn't have an obvious bruise for people to gossip about. She really wanted the boys in school but David Lee would just say he needed 'em at home. "Schoolin' ain't important. Learnin' to work is what really matters," he would say.

Most of the time, she just stayed home, only going into town for a few groceries at Crawford's Store when David Lee would give her a few dollars. She hated to ask for credit. Hazel had pride, too. She knew that this was no life either for her or for her children but there was no choice. It had to get better was her only hope. She wasn't really sure when she had stopped loving him.

"I'm tired of listenin' to all those folks and their braggin'," he told her when they were on their way home. "They all think that tobacco is the answer to their problems. Won't listen to David Lee. No sir! They all know more than old David Lee! Tobacco is nothing but constant work. Puttin' it on the bed, takin' it off, workin' in it through the summer, hoping that it don't get the blue mold or nothin'. Then you gotta stake it out and get it in the barn afore frost. Yeah, ain't nothin' but trouble. Now my still, why it ain't nothin' but pure pleasure. All a man has to do is throw a little corn in it, stoke the fire, and sit back and wait for the good stuff to flow. You shore outta be proud that your man done found hisself a good job and ain't breakin' his back in that old tobacco," he said as he pulled a pint jar of clear liquid from under the seat. "Guess I make the best corn mash whiskey in these parts, Hazel. You outta be proud of your old man," he bragged, taking a long swig. All Hazel could do was look out the dust stained window and nod. She knew it would only make things worse if she dared open her mouth.

"Yeah, they think they know it all. Think I can't hear 'em talk about old David Lee. Showed them Crawfords a thing or two. Don't need no list to sell pups. Not good pups like them. Old Frank Hester over at Hendersonville could see their breedin right off. Paid top dollar he did," he rambled on, taking another swig from the mason jar.

What could he possibly be talking about now, Hazel wondered as she looked into the back of the truck at her three prize possessions. "Please, God, don't let my boys feel his wrath tonight," she silently prayed.

CHAPTER 6

OLD SAM

ALL THE WAY HOME from the Ramp Convention, Pa kept telling Ma that he had waited too late to start plowin the tobacco field. "Henry Wiggins has already got his field ready. Says he's gonna' start settin' the first. I was tryin to wait until Mort comes home to help out but we just can't wait that long. I was gonna' be ready to start putin it in the field on the 10th but Henry says that's too late cause the signs won't be right."

"I know how you men think Henry Wiggins knows everything when it comes to tobacco, R.L., but I wouldn't worry none. If you get the ground ready in the next couple of weeks, I'm sure that it will be fine to start plantin on the 10th just like you always have. Mort's suppose to be home on the 12th, and until then, you won't have enough help to get it in the ground. You gotta remember that Lil' Jim, Joe and Matt are still children. They can help, but they are children, R.L.," Vadie tried to reassure him. And that's the way it was all the way home, Pa all worried like and Mama sayin everything would be all right.

Don't ever let anybody tell you that growin' tobacco is easy. First, you have to put it on the bed. That means that you plow, fertilize, and plant the tobacco seeds early in the spring; usually about the middle of March and cover the whole thing with a big, white muslin cloth to keep the frost out and the seeds warm. It kinda does look like a great big white bed out in the field.

When the plants get about three to four inches high, you take off the cloth so the sun can shine right on 'em. Then along about May 10th, after the last frost and when they're about six to eight inches tall, you pull 'em up and set 'em out again in the big field that has been plowed, fertilized, and got ready.

It seems like all summer long you gotta do somethin or other to them. In July, they bloom on the top and you have to pull it off so the leaves will get real big and thick. Then you have to pull off shoots that grow out where you don't want 'em to...that's called suckering. And you always have to watch out for the Blue Mold disease and worms and stuff. Then there's hoeing and keeping the weeds out. It's a whole lotta work.

About the first of September, it's time to harvest. That's when you have to put long sticks in the ground all over the field. Then when you cut the plants down with a big blade axe, you poke the big end of the stem over the stick...you put about six or eight plants on every stick and leave 'em out there so they can wilt. They stay out there for about a month or so. Then you have to gather them up and hang them in the barn to finish curing. When they get all dried out, you have to take 'em down and pull all the leaves off the stems. The big bottom leaves are placed in one pile, the middle leaves in another, and then the small leaves in another...cause you get a lot more for the little leaves than for the big 'uns...which don't make no sense. Looks like the bigger the better.

Then along about the middle of November, all the farmers take their crop to auction in Asheville. They all hope that this is a good year and that the tobacco companies will pay top dollar so they can pay their bills, taxes and mortgages for another year and maybe have a little left over for Christmas. And that's the way it goes around here, year after year, farm after farm. Everybody prayin for the same thing.

"Boys, we're gonna' get that field ready to plant. I'll need you all to stay home tomorrow. Maggie, you and Betty can go on to school. We'll need you more later. Just need the boys for a couple of days, tell Mr. Riley," Pa told us as we drove up the road after the Ramp Convention.

When we pulled up to the house, Nathaniel Putnam was sitting on the back step, hat in hand. He didn't look anybody in the face as he stood up and dusted off the seat of his britches. "Afternoon, Mr. Crawford. Miz Crawford."

"Afternoon, Nathaniel," Pa answered as he got out of the truck and stepped toward the visitor. "Vadie, take the girls in the house."

The women folk did as they's told while the rest of the Crawford clan just starred at the stranger standing in our yard.

"My Pa says that you're a fair man, Mr. Crawford. Says that you wouldn't hold to no cross burnin'. You treat folks fair and square." Nathaniel stumbled to get the words out, all the while lookin' at the ground and twistin' his hat round and round.

"That right, Nathaniel? Your Pa's a good man hisself. Don't reckon that I've ever heard anybody have anything bad to say about Ned or Susie Putnam."

"Thank ye' Mr. Crawford. It's been hard on him and Ma these last few weeks. Figure it's time I pulled my share of the load. He said that your oldest boy had done gone and joined the Army and that you was short handed. Wondered if you could use some help?"

"I am a little short, Nathaniel. Mort's due in but don't know if he'll be here when I need him. You ever worked tobacco?"

"No sir," he answered slowly. "But I got a strong back and I'm willin'."

"Guess we could try you out. It would just be until we get the crop in the ground. Can't pay much and you'd have to work hard. I don't put up with no slackers. Can you be here in the morning about day break?"

"No sir, I understand. I mean, yes sir. I'll be here. I won't cause no trouble either. I'll put in a good day. Thank you, Mr. Crawford." And with that, Nathaniel put his hand out, looked Pa in the eye and almost smiled.

They shook hands and Nathaniel Putnam just about skipped down the road.

"Don't know about that, Pa," Andy said when Nathaniel was out of sight. "You don't reckon it'll bring trouble, do you? Ain't no body seen 'em but Jimmy Ray says that Klan bunch is still around. Been meetin' up in the woods behind Claude Wright's. Jimmy Ray says they're adding' new members all the time and they're just bidin' their time. Waitin' to see what happens."

"Everybody deserves a chance, Andy. Ain't no man gonna find fault with that—Klan or no Klan." was all that Pa had to say. Everybody made their way back to the house.

NO ONE SAW HER SLIP OUT of the house and make her way to the barn; waiting for the young man to pass.

"You gonna work for my Pa? You ever done farm work before? My brother, Mort, is in the army. He was a good worker. You ever been in the army?" Questions just kept spilling out and the boy just kept walking. "What did you say your name was? Nathaniel? Like in the Bible? I gotta Bible name, too. Not Betty. My real name is Elizabeth Ann Crawford. You got a middle name?" She kept questioning and he kept walking, a little faster now. His long strides made it almost impossible for Betty to keep up. "You sure don't talk much, do you? I ain't never seen anybody that don't talk. My brother, Joe, he don't talk much either cause he's got this stutter. But at least he talks some. You stutter? Is that why you don't talk?"

"I gotta git on home," he finally answered. "You'd better be getting back to your folks." He began running and left her staring after him.

OUR MULE IS NAMED OLD SAM. He's the biggest, blackest mule anybody in these parts has ever seen, but he's a stubborn cus, too. Reckon that's why the owner wanted to sell him. We got him a couple of years back when Pa and Mort went over to the county livestock yard. Pa and Mort couldn't get him in the back of our truck to bring him home. Stubborn cus just wasn't about to get up in that truck bed. So Mort had to sit on the tailgate holdin his bridle and Old Sam walked all the way from the livestock yard to the farm and that's a fer piece.

He is one of the hardest working mules that anybody has ever saw. He'll walk in front of that plow all day, real steady down one row and back up the other. But the man that sold him to Pa told him, "Sam will pull a plow or sled all day and never stop; but don't never let nobody try to ride him. He won't let nobody on his back."

We worked all day. Old Sam must've gone up and down those rows at least a hundred times and he was almost white with sweat dropping off him like he'd been in the river. The tobacco had been on the bed since the middle of March and the plants were almost eight inches high and ready to be planted in the field.

Pa unhooked the plow and told Andy, "Take Old Sam to the other side of the barn and put him in the fence. The rest of you go on to the house and get cleaned up. We've all put in a good days work here. Nathaniel, you did a good job. You go on home and get a good night's sleep. We've got another hard day tomorrow."

"Yes, Sir, Mr. Crawford. I'll be here in the morning'."

And with that he headed down the road, rubbin' his back.

Andy thought that this was the perfect time to teach that mule a lesson. Old Sam would be too tired and worn out to do anything but let him ride and he was going to do just that. "Watch this!" he told the rest of us as were making our way toward the barn. "I'm gonna' ride this mule."

"You'd better not! He'll buck you off and Pa'll be madder than a hornet!" Matt told him as we reached the fence. "Sides that you ain't got no saddle."

"Don't need one. Just keep an eye out for Pa," Andy instructed as he opened the gate and led Old Sam inside while all the time rubbing his nose and talkin real quite in his ear.

Joe and me climbed on the rail to get a good look. Matt went around to the other side and climbed up where he could watch out for Pa. It was just like bein' at the rodeo. Andy whispered something in Old Sam's ear and rubbed him under his chin before he climbed on. "See, this ain't so bad! Told you I could do it!" he yelled as the mule just stood there for what seemed like a minute. But then, all of a sudden, Old Sam reared up on his front legs and gave one great, big kick with both his hind legs and slung Andy right over his head. Andy's arms and legs was going in all different directions and he must have cut three somersaults in the air. On the way down, Andy's forehead hit Old Sam's head right above his eye. Andy just kinda crumbled to the ground and lay there in a heap. Knocked him out cold as a wedge, it did.

"Get up Andy! Get up! Are you all right? Somebody get Pa!" we screamed as we scrambled off the fence. But Andy just lay there in the mud; still as could be with Old Sam just lookin' down at him. Andy didn't look like he was even breathing, with his eyes rolled back in his head and mouth gapped open.

"Come quick Mama! Come quick Mama! Old Sam's done kilt Andy! He was gonna' ride him and Old Sam bucked him off and kilt him!" Matt yelled and screamed as he ran toward the house. Me and Joe just stood over Andy, looking down at him laying there flat on his back and not knowing what to do.

Old Sam just stood there, too, as if to say, "You shouldn't try to mess with me, boy. I may be old and tired but I can still handle a little whippersnapper like you."

"What goin on here?" Pa yelled running around the corner of the barn sweat dripping off his chin.

Me and Joe both started crying, and screaming, "Old Sam's kilt Andy! Old Sam's kilt Andy! What do we do, Pa? Andy got on Old Sam and was gonna' ride him. What do we do?"

Pa kneeled over Andy and lifted his head out of the dirt with one of his calloused hands. We knew he was just as worried as we were as he began rubbing the mud off Andy's face. "Talk to me boy. Talk to me. You're gonna' be all right! What did you have to go and do a fool thing like that for?" Pa fussed and shook Andy's shoulders. But Andy didn't, or couldn't move. He just lay there limp as a wet dish rag.

Mama was on the back porch when she heard the commotion and started running toward us. Maggie and Betty weren't far behind. They ran past Matt running around in circles throwing his hands in the air and screaming, "Andy's dead! Andy's dead! Old Sam's done kilt Andy!"

Mama stopped at the water trough and picked up a bucket of water and when she got to Andy and Pa she threw it on the both of 'em. Andy began to moan and groan and his eyes started flittering but he still just lay there across Pa's arm and didn't move. "R.L., you and the boys get him up and move him to the back porch before he drowns in that mud! He's just got the breath knocked outta him. Lil' Jim, you run and get some rags to clean him up. I'm not lettin all that mud and dirt in my clean kitchen. I can't believe that you let him try to get on that old mule, R.L. You're as crazy as he is if you think Old Sam's gonna' stand by and let somebody on him."

"But, Vadie, I didn't...." Pa tried to defend himself.

"Don't 'but Vadie' me, R.L. You'll not be having nothing but milk and bread for supper for a week. None of you. Now get that boy to the porch! Y'all ought to be ashamed for scaring the life out of me like that," she said as she stomped back toward the house. "And somebody put that poor old mule in the barn and give him something to eat. He's worked hard all day, then y'all go and try some fool thing like this. Everyone of you ought to be ashamed. Maggie, you and Betty come on back to the house and bring Andy some clean clothes to the porch. I don't want him ruining my clean floors."

"Where's Nathaniel?" Betty asked, looking around. "He already gone? I want to ask him some questions."

"Yeah, he's gone. Guess he don't need to hear any more of your fool questions. You leave that boy alone, you hear," Pa answered a little short. "Now git on back to the house like your Mama said."

We all knew that we'd better do as Mama said, even Pa. Nobody wanted just milk and bread for supper. Andy may wished he'd really been kilt when Mama gets through with him. Nobody tried to get on Old Sam after that.

CHAPTER 7

A GIFT FROM THE HEART

WE ALL GO TO HAZELGROVE GRAMMAR SCHOOL
until we get in the ninth grade. It's a big, brick, two story
building on the edge of town. There's two classes in each
grade. Everybody whose last name starts with "A" through
"L" is in one class and the "M" through "Z's" is in the other
class. It's always been done that way. Don't matter none if
you're smart or not, you just go in the class where your
behind name falls in the alphabet. Grades one through four
are on the first floor and fifth through eight are on the top
hall. The cafeteria is in the basement along with the library.
When the teacher takes your class to the library, and you
find a book, you sit at one of the lunchroom tables until it's
time to go back to the room. There's a big playground out
back and a ball field over to one side. The front yard is just
grass and some big old Oak trees where the big girls sit and
talk about the boys.

Lots of people quit and don't go on to the high
school. Most are needed to work on the farms or some go
to work in the plant to help out their family. But I'm goin
to high school. My Mama says so. She got real mad when
Brother Mort quit in the 10th grade. Said that none of her
other young 'uns was gonna' do that if she had to march
them right into school ever day with a hickory stick to their
legs.

Mort looked real good when he was home this month on leave. He come walkin' up the road in his new Army suit. Mama cried and told him he's the most handsome Crawford that she's ever seen and that she bets all the girls in town will be writin' him letters when he goes back. Pa just told him to change his clothes that they had work to do. But every night he let Mort take the truck to town and he ain't never done nothing like that afore. Mort let me wear his hat. It's kinda funny. Folds up flat when you take it off. Maybe I'll join up and get me one of those nice suits when I'm old enough.

Right now, I'm in Miz Ginny Frady's fourth grade. I'm one of the oldest in my class, ten goin' on eleven, cause my birthday is so late in the year. My Mama says that's all right though, cause it don't matter none where or when you start, just that you finish. Our principal is Mr. Frank Riley and we're all real scared of him. He whips you with a leather razor strap if you don't mind. Now, I've never seen it but it must be true cause my brother Andy came home one day with red stripes on his legs and my Pa went down to the school and talked to Mr. Riley. When he got back home, he took Andy out behind the barn and whupped him again. You coulda heard him yellin' all the way down to Daddy Robert's store. Never did find out what Andy done to get whupped twice but I stay as far away from Mr. Riley's office as I can.

Miz Frady lets me and Harvey Brown, who's my best friend besides Joe, do special stuff for her. We dust the erasers out behind the building every afternoon and wash off the blackboards to get ready for the next day. Sometimes we even get to help Mr. James, our janitor, empty the trash.

The biggest boy in our class is Russell, Russell Gibson. He's real big but I don't know how old he is. Andy says that Russell was in Miz Frady's room when he was in fourth grade and that sure was a while back. Miz Frady always has him sit in the back of the room in the last desk nearest the window cause he kinda smells bad. It's real hard for him to fit in his desk cause he so tall so he has to kinda hunker over and bend his knees under his seat. Miz Frady always keeps the window open, even in the wintertime. Don't think he takes many baths, not even on Saturday. He wears the same shirt and overalls everyday. In the wintertime, he has a coat and a big pair of brown boots. They're both way too big for him but he don't seem to mind none. He don't wear his boots when the weather gets warm, he goes barefoot. I like to go barefoot, too, but my Mama makes me wear shoes to school.

I'm not sure just how smart Russell is cause he never speaks up or tries to answer Miz Frady's questions about 'rithmetic or social studies. He just keeps his head down and looks at the pictures in his readin book. He's been lookin at that same readin book all year. Sometimes Miz Frady has one of the girls that reads real good go sit with Russell and read to him. They all hate that a lot but Russell must really like it. That's about the only time I've ever seen him smile.

"Harvey, I'm gonna' ask Miz Frady if I can read to Russell sometime."

"Shoot, Lil' Jim, you must be crazy to want to sit next to that big, old dumb bell. You'll have to put a clothespin on ya nose just to breathe. There ain't no way I'd git that near him."

"Well, I'm gonna' ask anyways cause I like to see Russell smile. It ain't gonna' be that bad," I hoped.

Miz Frady said that it was mighty admirable of me to want to read to Russell and why didn't I do it that very afternoon. I waited until after I had finished all my 'rithmetic and then got out my favorite library book about a boy named Tom and his dog, Scout. When I pulled up a chair next to Russell's desk, he didn't even look up. Just kept starring at his reading book. Guess he didn't know I'd come to read. But as soon as I started, he just looked at me real strange like, closed his eyes, and settled back in his desk. Before I had finished the second page, Russell was smiling. Guess he liked my book, too. But it didn't take me long to finish the story—I kinda hurried cause he did smell something awful. I pushed my chair back and started to go back to my desk. Russell put one hand on my arm and the other one in his overall pocket. I'd never seen anything like what he pulled out. It was a small, wood dog; carved out all smooth and slick. He stuck it in my hand, smiled great big, and nodded his head but never said a word. I really wasn't sure just what I was suppose to do with it but I knew that it sure was somethin special. It looked just like Queenie, Pa's bird dog, with long curved legs and a skinny tail that stuck out straight—like when she was on the point. Somebody sure had a knack with a pocketknife to turn out something so fine. After admiring it for a spell, I put it back on Russell's desk, 'n turned to leave, "That's a mighty fine dog," I told him.

Then a miracle happened. Russell spoke. "It's your'n," and he put it back in my hand. Now I was plum bumfuzzled. Shucks, I didn't know what I was supposed to do. I sure did like that dog but I ain't sure what my Mama would say about me takin' something from somebody that was worse off than me. But I was sure that Russell meant for me to have it. And I sure didn't want to make him mad or nothing. So I took it and put it in my pocket until I had more time to think on it.

That afternoon, walking home from school, I told Joe that I had a special secret and that he couldn't tell nobody till I figured out what to do. "Cross your fingers and hope to die?"

"P..p..promise," and he held up his crossed fingers. When he saw the small wood dog, he was as surprised as I had been. "Did y..y..you s...s...steal this from s..s..omebody?" he stammered.

"No, how can you say that. It was give to me."

"W.w..who would give you s..s..such a fine thing?"

"Russell Gibson."

"R..r..russell Gibson? There ain't no w..w..way. W..w..w..who did he s..s..steal it from?" Joe finally was able to get out as he kept rubbing and turning the dog every which way.

"I don't know. Besides, how do you know he stole it? Maybe it's just his," I told him with as much of a certain voice as I could muster.

Joe just kept looking at the little wood dog. "A.a.a.a.ain't no way Russell Gibson would have nothing as fine as this. W..w..why, he don't even wear shoes to school m..m..most of the time. And why on earth w.w.w.would he give it to you?"

"Cause I read him a story bout a dog and he liked it! So just give it back and you'd better not tell nobody," I warned. "Don't you think it kinda looks like Queenie?"

He handed it back and I carefully put it in my pocket. "I won't t..t..tell but you k..k..know Mama's gon...na f..f..find out and be real mad." All the rest of the way home, Joe just kept humming to his self, "Lil' Jim's gonna' be in trouble." And all the rest of the way home I couldn't help but wonder how in the world Russell Gibson could have such a grand thing and how was I gonna' tell Mama. Joe was probably right. I was certain that Mama would march me down to school the next day and make me give it back, right in front of everybody.

I waited until after supper and all the chores were done and everybody had finished their homework. We were all getting ready for bed when I sneaked into the kitchen where Mama was getting pinto beans ready to soak over night so we could have them the next day. "Lil' Jim, why aren't you in bed? It's getting mighty late. Have you said your prayers?"

"I'm goin, Mama. But first, I gotta ask you somethin." I tried to think of just the right words. "If somebody gives you somethin, like a present, and it's not even Christmas or your birthday, are you suppose to take it?" I asked certain what the answer was going to be.

"Well, it depends, Lil' Jim. If you do something to earn it and they can't pay you, then I suppose it would be all right. Or if somebody thinks you've been a good boy and gives you something small, like Daddy Robert gives you a sucker at the store sometimes, then you should take it. But you know, Lil' Jim, you're always suppose to say thank you. Why, did someone give you something?"

"Yes, mam. But I didn't earn it and I don't think he thought I was a good boy," I told her as I handed her the beautiful dog from behind my back. "Ain't it wonderful, Mama? Don't it look like Queenie?"

"Don't say ain't, Lil' Jim. You know better and where in the world did you get this?" she asked, as she took the carving from my hand and looked it over, turning it ever which way.

"Russell Gibson give it to me," I tried to explain.

"Russell GAVE it to you? But why? And where do you think he got it?"

"He got it out of his overall pocket. And I'm not sure why he give it. I asked Miz Frady if I could read him a story and when I got finished, he just handed me this here little dog. Tried to give it back, Mama, honest, I did. But he wouldn't take it. Just handed it back to me. Kinda looks like Quennie, don't it, Mama? You ain't mad are you, Mama?"

"No, Lil' Jim, I'm not mad. Just confused and yes, it does look a little like Queenie. It was a very special thing that you did to read to Russell and I'm sure that he was very grateful. But I just can't imagine where he would get such a fine woodcarving. When you go back to school tomorrow, I want you to tell him that you really appreciate his gift but that you really can't take something that is so fine. That ever who gave it to him would be mad if they knew that he had given it away. Now, go on to bed, Lil' Jim. And tomorrow, I want you to mind your Mama, promise?"

"Yes, mam, I promise," I whispered not knowing just how I was suppose to do that. How was I gonna' talk to Russell. He never talked to nobody before today that I know of. He might not say anything back or worse, he might get mad and try to hit me. I'm littler than he is and probably quicker, but he sure is big! And what if some of the other kids see me talking to him and start joshin'. Glad I didn't tell Harvey about this mess cause he probably woulda told everybody. Boy, I sure did get myself in a heap of trouble just for asking to read to Russell.

Morning didn't come quick enough. I couldn't sleep. Just kept thinkin and tryin to figure just how to talk to Russell with out anybody knowin I'm talkin to him. I'm probably as tired this morning as I was when I went to bed last night. Sometimes it just don't pay to do stuff.

The morning was just like usual. We had reading, then 'rithmetic. Russell just sat at his desk in the back like always. I decided that the best time was when everybody went out side for recess. Most of the time during recess, Russell just goes over and leans against the building. He don't try to play ball or nothin'. Nobody ever chooses him to be on their team anyways.

I waited until all the boys were playin ball and the girls were jumpin rope before I sneaked over to Russell's spot and pulled the gift outta of my pocket. "This is a mighty nice dog and I really like it a lot but my Mama said I had to give it back. She said that who ever give it to you would be real mad if you give it away. So here," I said as I tried to put it in his dirty hand.

"It's yourn'. Nobody give it to me. Made it," he stated very matter of fact.

"You made it?" I was really amazed. "But how in the world…."

"Make lots of 'em. Coons, rabbits, squirrels, bears and such. Don't take much, just this here pocketknife and a little bit of wood. Nobody ever read to me cause they wanted to, but just cause Miz Frady makes 'em. Ain't got much but I want you to have it." About that time, the bell rang to go back inside.

Guess that's about the best present that I ever got. Mama says I can keep it. Said it was give from the heart and that's the best kind.

I showed it to Pa and he thinks it looks like Queenie, too. We put it on the mantle in the sittin room to remind us of her. Sometimes I like to take it down and just hold it and try to figure how somebody like Russell Gibson could make such a thing with nothin but a stick of wood and a pocketknife. Mama says that the Lord gives everybody a talent and guess this is Russell's. I ask her when she reckoned the Lord would give me my talent. She just laughed and said He already has and I'd find out what it was one day.

CHAPTER 8

OLD MAN HENSON'S CAVE

THE LAST DAY OF SCHOOL IS ALWAYS THE BEST day there is. First, you only have to go for half a day and you don't have to do reading, arithmetic, or nothin cause it's field day. That's where you get to go outside and everybody's on a team and you have contests. There's a jump rope contest for the girls to see who could jump the most times without missing. Jenny McClure won that. There's a baseball throw to see who can throw a baseball through an old tire that's hung from a tree by a rope. Billy Foster won that. Me and Harvey came in second the three-legged race. Our neighbor, Hank Hall, won the sack race and Joe came in second. There's lots of other races and such but the last thing is the tug-of-war. Joe, Hank, Harvey, and me were all on the same team but we didn't win. Everybody got a ribbon, though. Boy, it sure was a fun day.

Miz Frady rang the bell for us to go inside and get our report cards and stuff. Then she told Harvey and me to go dust off the erasers for the last time. Chalk dust filled the air as the erasers left white patterns on the side of the brick building. "What you gonna' do this summer, Harvey? Go fishin?" I asked, as we were about to finish up.

"Yeah, I'll probably fish some. But first, I'm gonna' find Old Man Henson's Cave," he answered still pounding the eraser.

"Now how do you think your gonna' do that? Ain't nobody ever found it."

"Yeah, but nobody's ever had a map afore," Harvey said and began pulling a dirty, torn piece of paper from his pocket. "Promise you won't tell, Lil' Jim. Cross your fingers and hope to die."

"Promise!" I said real fast trying to get a look at that paper Harvey had unfolded. "Where'd you get that?"

"My brother, Sam, got it down in Walnut from one of Old Man Henson's kinfolk. He sold it to me for a quarter. Goin up on Spivey Mountain next Saturday and find it. You'll see," he answered as we both stared at the homemade map, the erasers forgotten.

"What are you boys lookin at?" Matt asked as he and Lem Hall came around the edge of the building both with a handful of erasers. "Let us see."

"Ain't nothin. Sides, it's none of your business," Harvey said as he tried to stuff the map back in his pocket.

"Looked like a map to me, Matt," Lem said as he got near to Harvey. "What's it a map of Harvey? A gold mine or something?"

"Ain't no gold mine. Somethin' better than that. If I show you, you gotta promise not to tell. Promise?" He asked them both before getting the paper back out.

"I promise. I promise," they both answered quickly wanting to get a better look at just what Harvey had in his pocket.

"It's a map to Old Man Henson's cave. And I'm gonna' find it Saturday," Harvey bragged. He straightened the paper out again and everybody gathered around to get a close look. "My brother got it from one of Old Man Henson's kin and he sold it to me for a quarter. It's real and I'm gonna' be rich."

"Looks real to me," Lem said. He couldn't take his eyes off the paper. All the erasers lay in a heap at their feet, forgotten. "Let me go with you Saturday. Why, I've been up on Spivey afore with my Pa. Clear to the top, too. Bet I could find it."

"Yeah, you otta let us go along and help you," Matt volunteered, trying to get a closer look.

"Well, I don't know," Harvey was a little hesitant. "It's my map. Had to pay for it."

"Yeah, but it'll be a whole lot easier to find if you have help. And if it's just us that goes, and we find the cave and his treasure chest, there'll be plenty to go around," Matt tried to convince Harvey.

"Yeah, we'll all help you find it and you can keep the biggest share," Lem said with dollar signs in his eyes.

Harvey thought over their offer. I could tell he really didn't want to go up on Spivey Mountain by himself but he really hated sharing the money. "Ok, ok. But remember, I get to keep the most money. Promise?" Everybody nodded approval as they could think of nothing but being suddenly rich. Harvey carefully folded the paper and put it back in his overall pocket. "I gotta do chores first but we'll all meet at Crawford's store at 9:00 sharp, Saturday morning. Agreed? And no more. I ain't splitin it with no more. And if you ain't there, I'm leavin' without ya."

The heads of all three boys just kept bobbing up and down and they kept thinking, "We are gonna' be rich."

Just one more won't matter. I'll have to tell Joe. Harvey won't care if Joe comes along. Sides, I'll share my part with Joe.

As the story goes, old man Henson, an army deserter from the First World War, was a rich man who didn't believe in banks. Kept all his money in a big trunk. He was from around these parts but knew that he couldn't go back home after he deserted, so he found a cave up on Spivey Mountain and lived there. The soldiers and police would come a lookin for him from time to time but could never find him cause the brush was so thick you could hardly walk and there were rock cliffs everywhere. His kinfolk would leave food in an old hollow tree at the foot of the mountain and he would sneak down and get it. Folks say that he hid his big trunk full of money in that cave.

He stayed up on that mountain 10 years. People would see him from time to time after dark when he would sneak into town. Said he was real scary lookin and that livin like that had made him plum crazy. Then, one day, he stopped comin down and gettin the food that was left for him. Nobody ever knew what happened. Some say he most likely fell off a cliff and died. But that trunk of money is still suppose to be up there in that cave. Lots of people have looked but nobody has ever found it. But they didn't have a map either.

Mama says she don't like her boys goin' traipsing off to look for something that's not there. "That's just an old tall tale, boys. You're not gonna' find anything. Besides that, it's dangerous up there on that mountain. One of you could fall and get hurt or killed."

"But Mama, we'll be real careful. There'll be five of us and we won't take no chances. It'll be fun, like an adventure. Like Tom Sawyer and Huck Finn," begged Matt.

"Yeah, M..m..mama, it'll be l..l..like an adventure," Joe piped in. We all begged and promised and begged and promised until Mama had no choice if she ever wanted us to shut up.

"Ok, ok, you all can go if you get your chores done first. But you had better be back here before dark," she finally gave in. "And you had better look after each other, too. You hear me, boys?"

We could hardly sleep Friday night for thinking about our adventure. There were whispers until way into the night. Finally, when it was morning, we quickly did all our chores, grabbed our bag of peanut butter and jelly sandwiches that Mama had made and were at Daddy Robert's store at exactly 9:00. Lem and Hank were already there sitting on the steps. They didn't have a bag of sandwiches. They said that their Pa told 'em they couldn't go, that they had to work. But their Mama had come to their bed last night and told them to sneak off early, she'd take care of their Pa.

Nathaniel was sweepin' off the porch and steps of the store—getting' ready for the Sit n' Spit fellers, I reckon. He'd started workin' at the store right after we got the tobacco in the ground. Daddy Robert said he was good help keeping stuff straight and all. Said all he ever done was nod to the customers—most didn't know if he could even talk.

Harvey came runnin' down the road. He'd been runnin' so hard, he bout couldn't catch his breath and had to bend over and grab the legs of his overalls. I could tell he didn't much like it that now there were six of us that would have to share the money. But he said it was OK when I told him that me and Joe would only take one share. Lem and Hank said they'd do the same.

"OK. But you all just remember that when it comes time to divey it up. We'd better get out of here before the whole town wants to come along and nobody will get nothin'."

Mama Annie came to the door of the store and wanted to know just what we were doing there so early? We told her not to tell anybody, but we were going up on Spivey Mountain to find Old Man Henson's cave.

"Nobody should go off on such an trip on an empty stomach. Here get you one of these cookies for the road and put another one in your bag," she told us as she handed out the still warm goodies.

"Thank you Mama Annie. When we come back with all that money, we'll buy all your cookies," I told her as I took a nibble.

"Yeah, thanks!" everyone chimed in, waving good-bye.

"My Pa says your pa and grandpa better watch their back," Harvey told the Crawford boys as they started down the street. "Says the Klan'll be back and burnin' crosses your yard if you keep rubbin' elbows with that Nathaniel and his kind."

"Oh, Harvey, you don't know what your talking about," Matt answered for the other Crawfords. "Nathaniel ain't caused no trouble around here and he's good help. Why, everybody's knowed his Pa and Ma for a long time and their good folk."

"They may be good folk," Harvey continued, "but that boy ain't nothing but trouble. Folks don't like his kind around the women folk."

"You don't know what your talking about, Harvey," Matt told him matter-of-factly. "My Pa says everybody deserves a chance. Sides, that Klan ain't nothing but a bunch of sissies—sneakin' around in the middle of the night, hidin' behind them robes and masks. Bet their long gone from around here."

"Harvey's right, Matt. Most folks think he outta go back to where he come from. Don't like his kind and don't want 'em around here," Lem kinda whispered. "Wouldn't want nothing bad to happen to you all just because of him."

"Ain't nothing bad gonna' happen. And I don't want to hear nothing more about it and that's final!" Matt told them.

"Seen Betty talkin' to him a lot at your Grandpa's store. People are talkin'. She had better be careful, that's all I'm saying," Harvey added.

"Told you, don't want to hear any more about it. Betty's just being friendly. She'd talk to the devil hisself if she run into him. Now, leave it be. Don't want to hear any more," Matt insisted and moved on ahead of the group.

"Didn't mean to make Matt mad, Lil' Jim. Just thought you all would want to know what folks was sayin'. And they ain't gone either. Pa said he saw a bunch of 'em the other night up behind the Wright place," Harvey said as he stopped to check his pocket for the hundredth time.

"He ain't mad, Harvey. But like he said, 'nough said." I shore didn't want to spend the rest of the day thinking about a bunch of men runnin' around in white robes. We were gonna find Henson's cave and all be rich.

Now Spivey Mountain was way at the other end of town, past the barber shop and the bank, across the bridge and up the road where Granny Ruth lives. That my Mama's mama. Granny Ruth's the one everybody sends for when there's sickness or a baby 'bout to be born and they can't get Doc Prichard. She knows all about herbs and salves and poultices and such. She knows just what to give a colicky baby to make it stop crying or what to put on a cut or on a sore. Don't know nobody that likes her mouth medicine. It always tastes something awful and you're sure you're gonna' die. Don't know anybody that has—but know some that wished that they had cause it tasted so bad. Mama says that Betty takes after Granny Ruth with her knack of takin' care of hurt animals and stuff.

Her house is white and kinda small but it has a porch all the way across the front. There are a couple of rockin' chairs and a big swing and people are all the time stoppin' by just to set a spell and have a glass of sweet tea. Ain't nobody there this morning though. Too early, I guess.

The yard is always full of all kinds of flowers. There's pots of pink ones and yellow ones and red ones everywhere. I don't know what kind they are but they sure are pretty and smell real good. Everybody in town says that nobody can grow stuff like Granny Ruth.

"What you boys up to this morning?" Granny Ruth called, peeking out of the mass of color on the other side of her fence. "Y'all look like a bunch of rag-tag Reb soldiers looking for Yankees."

We all 'bout jumped out of our skin, 'cause nobody knowed she was there. "That's us, Granny Ruth. Lookin' for Yanks!" everybody called out, laughing. Everybody likes Granny Ruth.

Out beyond Chambers' apple orchard, we turned up this old dirt road that looked like nobody had been on it in years. Then the road just upped and stopped and there was nothing but a narrow trail. We climbed over rocks and felled trees and through laurel thickets as we made our way up the mountain. Harvey was leadin the way, then there was Matt and me and Joe. Lem and Hank were behind Joe. We musta climbed bout a mile when the trail just stopped. There were tall trees and laurel bushes and big old rocks everywhere but no trail.

"Get the map out, Harvey, so we can tell which way we're suppose to go," Lem told him while the rest of us found a rock to rest on after the hard climb.

"Give me a minute. Gotta catch my breath. No need to be in no hurry. That treasurer ain't goin' no place," Harvey told him as he wiped the sweat from his forehead with his hankie.

It was a beautiful, warm, June morning. Laying there on my back, I could look through the green leaves of the tall Oak trees and see the clear Carolina blue sky. The only thing breaking the silence, besides the birds chirping, was a woodpecker somewhere in a tree not far away finding his breakfast. It was hard not to dream about how I would spend my part of the loot, now that we were so close.

After a few minutes, Harvey carefully removed the paper from his overall pocket, straightened it out and lay it carefully on a big rock. We all gathered around where we could get the best look. "I think we are right here," Harvey said pointing to a spot on the paper. "See, here is Panther Creek and over here is that big rock cliff. We just have to get up over there and across that little holler and the cave should be right there."

"Yeah!" We all agreed getting our second wind. "It can't be too far. Let's get goin'. We're all gonna' be rich!" Everyone seemed to say at once. We all scrambled up to set off in the direction that Harvey had pointed to. By tonight, we were all gonna' be rich!

We climbed over steep rocks and had to pull each other up as we made our way toward the holler and what was sure to be old man Henson's cave. We had to crawl on our knees through the roughest mountain laurel thicket I've ever seen. About the time we all thought we were sure to be close, we had to go through a blackberry briar thicket.

"We could go around," Harvey said looking around and trying to find another way. "It'll be a little bit longer, but I just don't know if we can get through them briars."

"I don't want to go around. Might miss it and not be able to find the right spot if we go around," Matt stated. But no one really wanted to tackle those briars.

"Matt's right," Lem agreed. "I'll go first and push the briars out of the way. Then it won't be so bad. Can't be much further." Lem was the only one who had worn a shirt under his overalls. "Just follow me, boys," he said, proud to be the leader at last as he disappeared into the thick briar patch. Hank was only a couple of steps behind him with me and Joe and Matt just after him. Harvey brought up the rear.

"Ouch!" Harvey cried out as a vine whipped around his shoulder. "Maybe we ought to go around."

"Oh, come on Harvey, don't be such a baby!" Matt yelled back. "A little scratch ain't gonna' kill ya."

Despite the fact that their new leader tried to push the vines with their razor-sharp briars to the side, bloody scratches covered the boys' exposed arms. "How much further, Lem? Can you see anything?" Matt called out trying to get through the briars that Lem had pushed to one side.

"Can't see nothing but more briars. But we should be close. Can't be much farther," he called back to us and we kept going.

"Don't nobody move or say nothing," Lem whispered with fear and panic in his voice after only a couple of more steps. The line of boys suddenly became statues. What could it be we all wondered but didn't dare ask. The briars had snapped back putting Lem and Hank completely out of sight. I stood as still as I could with briars around my arms and legs and cutting into my face. We were all afraid to even breathe...could it be a bear?

Then, just as I was about to have to remove a briar that was sticking me in the cheek, Lem let out the worse scream that I've ever heard and started fallin back toward Hank. "Snakes! Snakes! Rattlers!" He yelled and screamed again. They both fell down and started rollin down the mountain with briars wrappin around them from head to toe. Joe, Matt and Harvey and I turned around and ran as hard as we possibly could not paying any attention to the terrible scratches that covered our bodies. The vines acted like whips as they wound around our arms and legs and didn't want to turn lose.

Clearing the briars, we all fell on the ground trying to get our breath. We looked like we had been in a dogfight and were bleeding from every spot on our body not covered by our overalls. "You all right? You all right?" Matt asked looking from one to the other. Completely out of breath, we could only nod. "Where is Hank and Lem? Lil' Jim, Joe, Harvey, where is Hank and Lem?"

"Oh!" someone moaned from behind us. "Oh!" it came again from over the edge of the big bank that seemed to drop off to nowhere.

"Can y'all see anything?" Matt asked when we had crawled over to the bank to look into the black.

"We're down here," a small voice floated up from the dark.

"We're comin! We're comin! Just hang on!" Matt yelled to them and scrambled over the edge and down the bank and through the thick growth. Not knowing what else to do, the rest of us followed Matt into the black hole.

Hank and Lem both lay bruised and bleeding, tangled up in briars. "Get us outta here! Get us outta here!" Hank cried, tears streaming down his face. But Lem just lay real quite, staring straight up but not looking at anything. "Ouch, that hurts! Don't pull so hard. Get your knife and cut 'em off," Hank begged as we tried to free them. But Lem didn't say a word. Matt got his knife out and slowly began cutting the briars away one at a time first from their neck and arms and then from their legs. As Matt cut the sharp daggers, Joe and I worked as gently as possible to pull them away. It's hard to believe that something so sweet and juicy can come from something so terrible. When we finally had them free, Hank stood up, took out his hanky and started dabbing at the blood on his arms. But Lem just lay still.

"You can get up now, Lem. Come on, I'll help you," Matt told him as he put his hand down for him to get a hold of. But still, Lem didn't move. "Come on, Lem. Let's get outta here."

"Been bit," was all he could manage and tried to point to his ankle. Matt pulled up the leg of his overalls and we saw something that looked real bad. It was already swollen up and fiery red all the way up to his knee. He had two small holes right above his anklebone that if you just didn't know you would have thought was just another briar prick.

"What are we gonna' do? What are we gonna' do?" Hank cried. "Don't die Lem! Don't die! Do something, Matt. Don't let Lem die!"

"I don't know…" Matt stammered. "I ain't never took care of no snakebite afore. I don't know what to do."

"Shut up your bawlin, Hank. That ain't helpin nothing!" Harvey shouted. "Now we just gotta think. Surely, we can think of something." But each one just stood with their mouth open staring at Lem's leg. It was hard to look but at the same time I couldn't look away.

"I saw Granny Ruth tie a rag around Big Jack's leg one time when he cut it," I offered.

"This ain't no cut leg, Lil' Jim," Harvey shot back.

"No, but it can't hurt. Everybody give me your hanky," Matt said as he took charge. He tied two of our hankies together and then wrapped them around Lem's leg just above the knee. Hank just sat staring at his brother, not moving, tears still streaming down his face.

"Granny Ruth tied them real tight and ever once in a while, she would let it loose for a minute and then tighten it again," I remembered. So Matt tightened the hankies around Lem's leg as he lay there not saying anything.

"Think you're suppose to cut it where the bite is and suck out the poison," Matt said. "Anybody know how to do that?"

"I sure don't!" Harvey said. "But I think that sounds right." It seemed that no one knew how to go about cutting the bite and sucking out the poison but we all felt that that was the right thing to do. No one could think of anything else to do but no one moved in case it wasn't the right thing.

"Joe, you get his other leg and hold it real tight. Hank, you get one arm and Harvey, you get the other. Lil' Jim, come round here and hold this foot real still. Now, Lem, I'm gonna' cut your leg a little and try to get that poison out. Can you take it?" Matt asked as we all got to our assigned spots.

"Just do it, Matt," Lem answered very weakly.

Matt found a small branch and put it in Lem's mouth. "Bite down on that 'cause it's gonna' hurt," he said as he wiped the knife blade off on his overall leg and sat down on the ground. I took hold of Lem's foot and put his leg across Matt's lap. He just kinda groaned. Everybody else took hold and we all held on real tight. Matt didn't say that I had to watch him do the cutting, so I didn't. But I knew when he did it because Lem gave a loud groan and jerked every part of his body. It didn't seem to take long before Matt leaned down and began to suck on Lem's leg and then he would spit out blood and poison. He did that for 8 or 10 times before he stopped and said that he reckoned that was about enough. As he tied another hankie around Lem's ankle where he had made the cut, Matt let out a long breath and continued to look at his work. It was as if he was afraid to look at Lem in the face or at anyone else...afraid that he had not done enough...afraid that he had done the wrong thing...afraid that his friend would die.

Hank was still crying but real low. "Is he gonna' die, Matt? Is Lem gonna' die?"

"Don't know. Just don't know," he answered trying to take hold of the situation. "But I do know that we gotta get him off this here mountain as fast as we can. Everybody get up! Lem, put your arm around my shoulder. Harvey, get his head and Joe get the other shoulder. Hank you and Lil' Jim get his feet. We're gonna' carry him down." Matt was still in charge.

"I don't think I can do that, Matt. He's too heavy," Harvey complained as we tried to pick him up as gently as we could.

"Well, we have to. There ain't no other way. We can't just leave him up here and send for help. It'd take too long. Now git his head, Harvey, and stop your belly achin'," Matt ordered. "We'll be as careful as we can Lem. You just hang in there. We're gonna' git you off this here mountain as quick as we can."

We all did as we were told again and walked, stumbled and fell down the mountain. Our load was heavy but Harvey didn't complain again or said that he couldn't do it and neither did anyone else. No one said a word. It seemed like it was a lot farther down that it had been going up. When we finally reached the dirt road, we sat down and gently leaned Lem up against a tree and tried to catch our breath.

"How you doin, Lem?" Matt asked as he wiped the beads of sweat first from Lem's face and then from his own. The rest of us were too afraid to look.

"How much farther?" was all he could manage to say. His face was as white as one of the hankies that was tied around his leg.

"Ain't far now. Gonna' git you help as fast as we can, Lem. You just hold on tight," Matt tried to reassure him all the while trying to not let anyone feel his fear. He realized that if he let a bit of doubt creep into his voice, the younger boys would panic and they would never get Lem to safety. "Lil' Jim, I need you to run on ahead and get Granny Ruth. Tell her what's happened. Let her call Daddy Robert at the store and get him to bring her up here. In the mean time, the rest of us will bring Lem down the road as far as we can. Now run, Lil' Jim. Run as fast as you can. I'm countin on you. Lem's countin on you."

"I'll do it, Matt!" I cried as I ran. It seemed more like fifty miles rather than two to Granny Ruth's house. What if I don't make it. What if Lem dies because I can't run fast enough. "Please don't let Lem die, God. Please don't let Lem die." I prayed with every step. Doubt kept racing through my head. "Granny Ruth, Lem's been snake bit," I shouted as I got to her front gate. "Come quick, Granny Ruth, come quick." I could barely breath. "Call Daddy Robert. Tell him to come in his truck."

Granny Ruth ran out onto her front porch wiping her hands on her apron. She was a short woman about as round as she was tall. She always had on a long white apron with smudges of grape jelly or apple sauce or what ever dotting it. "What are you hollering about, Lil' Jim? Just calm down and tell me what's wrong."

I tried to get my breath as I collapsed on her front steps. "Lem Hall's been snake bit!" I managed to get out. "Matt and Joe and Harvey and Hank are carryin him down the mountain. Please hurry Granny Ruth. Don't let Lem die! Call Daddy Robert to bring his truck and take us up there. Hurry Granny Ruth, hurry," I begged.

Granny Ruth hurried into her house and dialed up the store. I could hear her tell Daddy Robert that he needed to be quick. All I could do was lay across the steps and try to breathe. It wasn't but just a minute until she came out with her little bag, "Tell me where they are Lil' Jim!" she said as she began running across the yard.

"They're up on Spivey Mountain!" I yelled, getting up and running after her. I didn't know she could move so fast.

"Daddy Robert will be on in a minute. We'll go on ahead and he'll catch up. Do you want to wait and ride in the truck, Lil' Jim?" she asked still running.

"No, I'm gonna' go with you. Please, Granny Ruth, Lem ain't gonna' die is he?" I begged her to reassure me.

We had only gone about a quarter of a mile when I heard Daddy Robert's truck coming up the road behind us. He stopped only long enough for Granny Ruth to get in the front seat and for me to hop in the back on some feed sacks. I was really glad to get to lay down for a minute and catch my breath. I could hear Granny Ruth tellin Daddy Robert about the trouble. "Please, God, don't let Lem die," I prayed until we finally saw Matt and the boys carrying him down the road.

"Lay him right over here under this tree and y'all move away boys," she told them and they were only too glad to do as they were told. They carefully lay their load on the grass beneath a large oak tree. Then they each patted Lem on the shoulder before finding a spot to rest and watch. Granny Ruth was in charge now. She got some stuff out of her bag. Daddy Robert held Lem's head as she untied the hankie around Lem's ankle and put some kind of poultice on the bite and then bandaged it up again. She untied the hankies from around his leg and then tied them back again. She got some more medicine from her bag and gave it to Lem with a big jar of water. All the while, she was talking to him real "quite like" and he seemed to be lookin not as afraid. After a bit, she told us to lift him up into the back of the truck real easy and that Daddy Robert would take us all home.

"Is he gonna' be all right?" Hank asked her, needing to be reassured.. "Is he gonna' be all right?"

"We'll need to get him to a doctor, but I think he's gonna' be all right. I'm real proud of you all. How did you all know what to do?"

"It was Matt." We all answered at once and began tellin her about what had happened.

"Matt cut his leg and sucked out the poison," I told her. I was real proud of my brother.

"Well, Lem can thank Matt and the rest of you. Y'all saved his life. You should be real proud of yourselves. But you all don't look much better off than Lem with all those scratches. Now, get him in the truck so we can get him to his folks," she said patting each one of us on the head. We did just as we were told.

We stopped at Granny Ruth's long enough for her to call Doc Prichard and tell him to meet us at the Hall's house. Harvey got outta the truck, too, and said he reckoned he'd git on home. Guess he'd had enough adventure for one day.

I said another prayer as we drove, "Thank you, God. Thank you for not lettin Lem die. And thank you for lettin Matt know what to do."

The ride was bumpy but no one seemed to mind. Everybody stretched out on the grain sacks, lost in their own thoughts. This day sure had been an adventure all right.

"You boys get Lem out and carry him over to the house," Granny Ruth ordered when the truck stopped at the edge of the Hall's yard . Each adventurer took hold and gently helped Lem out of the truck. "Robert, let's see if we can find his Ma and Pa," she told him as they headed toward the house in front of the pack.

Mr. Hall came around the corner of the house just as we propped Lem up against the porch post. Daddy Robert turned toward him, "Your boy's been snake bit, David Lee. We've called Doc Prichard and he's on the way. Seems these boys been up on Spivey...."

"Y'all get on back! I'll take care of Lem. Got what he deserved sneakin off like that," He interrupted. "Hank, git on out to the barn, I'll deal with you later. Old man, git these people off my property. Don't need your help no more!" he scowled at us all.

Me and Joe and Matt couldn't get in the back of the truck fast enough. Granny Ruth tried to tell him that his boy was hurt real bad but Mr. Hall just gave her a real mean look and said, "Don't need you Crawfords tryin to tell us how to take care of our own. Now you heard me...git ."

Granny Ruth just shook her head as she slowly climbed back in the truck without saying a word. I think she prayed for Lem all the way back to our house. Daddy Robert didn't say nothin either. Guess we all had a hard time believing what we'd just heard.

None of us cared about going up to Spivey Mountain after that and we didn't much care about old man Henson's cave or his trunk full of money either.

CHAPTER 9

FIREWORKS

NOBODY HAS SAW ANY OF THE HALL BOYS since our adventure trying to find Old Man Henson's cave and that's been a whole month. Mrs. Hall has only come to church one Sunday this whole summer and that was right after Lem was snake bit. When preachin' was over, she came over to where me and Granny Ruth were sittin' and told her that she really appreciated her taking care of Lem and seein that he got home. She told her that Doc Prichard said he'd probably died or at least lost his leg if it hadn't been for her and us boys and she just wanted to say thanks.

Granny Ruth said that she was only too glad that she could help and was certainly relieved that he was going to be alright. "Prayers are answered," she told Miz Hall just before she slipped out the back door of the church.

Maybe the Halls will be at the Fourth of July celebration. Everyone else in town will certainly be there. It is the biggest holiday of the year exceptin for Labor Day. All the ladies will bring big baskets of fried chicken, potato salad, green beans, corn on the cob, biscuits, cornbread, and every kind of desert you can think of. Then there'll be watermelons! Lots of watermelons!

After lunch, everybody will gather around the big tent that's been set up in the middle of the field to listen to music. Church choirs, traveling musicians that are trying to get noticed in Nashville, or just anybody that wants to or thinks they can carry a tune, will come and sing country and gospel songs until after dark. Even Matt plans to take his guitar and get up there. He's been practicing for a month some Hank Williams' song that he heard on the radio. We're all getting kinda tired of hearing "*I'm So Lonesome I Could Cry*" from morning till night. He must be getting pretty good though. Been singin in the choir with Mama on Sundays. Why, he even sang a solo a couple of weeks back and after church everybody just kept slapping him on the back and tellin him what a fine job he'd done.

There'll be several bands so folks can square dance or buck dance. It is always a great day but the best part is always last… Fireworks! People will sit in the back of trucks or lay a quilt on the ground and watch as the sky is lit up with all kinds of colors. Blue, red and green with whistles and loud explosions. Me and Joe always like the Roman candles best. They go way up in the air and bust into at least a million sparkling lights…boom… boom…boom! I can hardly wait!

Seems like we've not had no time to do fun stuff this summer. Every day we have to help Mama in the garden. She always likes to have a big garden with all kinds of vegetables that she can put up for the winter. They sure do taste good when your eatin' 'em but I don't much like to hoe and stuff. Andy and Matt help Pa top and sucker the tobacco. Seems like there's always stuff that's gotta be done with it. And then there's the apple orchard; it's gotta be sprayed regular for bugs and worms. I heard Mama say "Woman's work is never done!" but I think it should be "farm work ain't never done." Why, I'll bet we ain't been to the Mease hole swimmin' more than five times and I ain't got to go fishin' but twice. But today's July Fourth and we ain't gonna' have to work today!!

"NOW, BETTY, I'VE ALREADY TOLD YOU several times, you're just too young to take a box lunch this year. Next year when you turn 14, that's soon enough," Mama told Betty again as she placed the fried chicken in a big basket. "Now, come and help me with the potato salad. If we don't get going, all the fun's going to be over before we ever get there."

"You think Nathaniel and his family will be there? Don't reckon I've ever seen his folks at the picnic. Why don't they come? Is it because they are colored?" Betty began her thousand questions.

Mama just looked at the ceiling and silently prayed, 'Please God just give me the answers.'

"Just because they look different don't mean they can't come and enjoy eatin' and fireworks like everybody else. Nathaniel's real nice once you get to know him. He even talks some."

"Probably not, Betty. Some folks wouldn't like it if they came. Wouldn't make 'em welcome," Mama answered as she wiped her hands on her apron. "Now are you gonna help me or not! I can't do this by myself."

"Yes, ma'am. But I still don't understand. Seems to me that folks is folks no matter what the color of their skin. And we outta be nice to 'em. Ain't that what the Bible says?" she continued not willing to let it drop. "Mama, you always say, 'Do unto others as you would have them do unto you.' That's what the Bible says. Not do unto others if their skin is the same, or they talk just like you do, or if their hair is the color of yours. Ain't that right?"

"Betty, I don't know where you get all your questions. Yes, that is right. Love one another. It's just that some people don't think that means everybody. We should be nice and friendly to all the Putnams. Yes, they are different but God made them, too. I am proud that you and Nathaniel have become friends. Just don't get too friendly so that people will have something to talk about. Now! I need some help, young lady."

"But, Mama, I don't...."

"That's enough. We've got work to do and it's almost time to go. Save your questions for another day," Mama scolded her youngest daughter. How could she possible explain that it was OK to be friends but where do you draw the line. Betty had been a chatterbox ever since she uttered her first word. She certainly did not want to quash her outgoing personality but she didn't want the people in town to start gossiping. She'd have to talk to R.L. Maybe he would have the answers. Or maybe her mother, Granny Ruth. She always knew the best way to solve problems before they could grow into mountains.

Maggie had been working on her box lunch for days. It had to be just right. She wanted to make sure that every boy in Hazelgrove will want to bid on it and that it will go for the highest price ever paid at the auction. You see, all the eligible girls in town fix up a basket or a small box and make it look real snazzy on the outside. On the inside, they'll put a nice lunch for two—enough for herself and whichever boy is the highest bidder. All the eligible young men will bid on the boxes, trying to figure out who's brought which one and who they're gonna' have lunch with. The money always goes for a good cause, but the girl has all the bragging rights for a year. It's always a big deal! At least to the girls.

"Here, Betty, you can help me, too. Put your finger right here so I can tie this big bow," Maggie ordered. "I'm gonna' have the best box at the auction this year, I just know. I sure do hope that Johnny Lee Hall is there. He'll bid on my box and maybe Tommy Joe Smathers will, too. I just hope I don't have to eat with old Bobby Thompson though. He always chews with his mouth open and grins and says the dumbest things that ain't at all funny. Then he laughs real loud like he's made the best joke." Maggie tied the big blue bow with streamers that hung down to the sides. She had wrapped the box in paper that Mama Annie had found in her attic. It was white with big blue dots.

"I sure don't see why you think Johnny Lee is so special. Never heard him say more than two or three words since I've known him. He just kinda stands around with his hat in his hand and his head down, lookin' at the ground. Shucks, I'd bet he'd probably jump right out of his skin if somebody said 'BOO' to him. And how's he gonna' bid on your box lunch if he don't talk…get one of his brothers to bid for him?" Betty teased, helping her with the bow. "I'd much rather eat with Bobby Thompson, at least he talks!"

"You don't know anything! Johnny Lee says a lot when he's around me. Maybe he just don't have anything to say to you cause you're still a child," Maggie shot back as she admired her handiwork and fluffed the bow one more time for good measure. "Yep, I'm gonna' have the best box at the auction this year."

"Girls, stop your picking at each other and get the rest of this stuff put in the back of the truck. It's time to go," Mama said as she hurried to the foot of the stairs. "Boys, have you all washed your face and hands? Are you ready? Let's go!" she called up the steps.

Down they all tumbled, wearing their best overalls, with faces and hands scrubbed clean and hair slicked back. All her boys looked very presentable, for the moment. Matt looked especially nice in his new western shirt that Granny Ruth had made him for his singing debut. It was blue plaid with white cording around the collar and cuffs and down the front. Daddy Robert had even ordered him a white western hat to wear. He really did look like a musician as he stood in the bathroom, taking one last look in the mirror and trying to slick down his red cowlick.

Vadie just wished her oldest son could be there to join in the fun. He would enjoy it the most of all, him being the social one in the family and all. Mort had never seen a stranger. Would probably walk up to the Devil, hisself, and ask him how he was doin'. She had only heard from him once since he had gone back. He was stationed somewhere up in Pennsylvania and he didn't know for how long. Still might have to go over seas, maybe to Korea, if they didn't get something worked out. The Post Master had told her that he really wasn't suppose to say, but "I think that pretty Peterson girl has got a few letters," Vadie would seek her out today. She'd try not to be too obvious but with a hint here and there, maybe she could find out something. Surely, Becky would be there with her family.

They had piled bales of hay in the back of the truck to sit on. It would be the perfect spot to watch the fireworks later that night. "Mama, can't I sit up front with you and Pa? I don't want to get my dress smelling all bad before we even get there." Maggie begged. She had spent half the morning trying to decide which dress was just the right one to wear and making sure her hair was just right. Mama scooted over to the middle and gave her room to climb in while everyone else pilled in the back.

"When we get there, I want y'all to help me find Granny Ruth first thing. She suppose to be riding over with the Hardins," Vadie told them as they bounced down the road. "I don't want everybody to go runnin' off in ever direction before we get all our stuff put out on the tables, you hear!"

"Yes, ma'am," came the chorus from the back of the truck.

MAGGIE CAREFULLY PLACED HER BOX on the long
auction table with the others. There were more boxes than
she had ever seen, must be at least 25 this year. She wasn't
sure that there would be enough eligible boys to bid on that
many. What if all the eligible boys bid and bought one
before hers even came up? She would be the joke of the
town if they ran out of bidders and she had to eat alone.
This is certainly something that she had not thought
of...wonder if that had ever happened before? She had to
come up with a plan and fast because Daddy Robert was
about to start the bidding. She had to make sure that
Johnny Lee or Tommy Joe knew which box was hers and
saved their bid.

"Come here, Lil' Jim. Come here. I need your help
just a moment, please," Maggie purred as she wandered to
where he was standing near Daddy Robert. "Happy Fourth
of July, Mama Annie and Daddy Robert. It sure is hot, isn't
it? I need to ask a favor. Lil' Jim, would you come over
here?" she pleaded, taking hold of his elbow and guiding
him toward the end of the tables.

"I'm busy, Maggie. What do you want?" he asked
jerking his elbow away and trying to watch Daddy Robert
get ready to auction off the boxes.

Maggie whispered in my ear, "I need you to find
Johnny Lee Hall or maybe Tommy Joe Smathers before the
bidding starts and show them which one is my box so they
can bid on it. I'll give you a nickel if you promise that you'll
find 'em, Lil' Jim." She looked around to see if anyone was
watching. "Don't tell nobody, though. They might think I
was cheatin or somethin. OK? Will you do that for me?"

"I don't even know if they're here or not. Not seen
'em. And why do they need to know which box is yours?

Thought they's suppose to just bid on any old box they want," I answered.

"I don't want to eat with just any old boy, Lil' Jim. Why, I might end up with old Mr. Hank Franklin! He's old enough to be our father. I sure don't want to have to eat lunch with somebody as old as him! Now, please, Lil' Jim. I'll make it a quarter if you'll just find them for me. Tell them that mine is the white one with big blue dots."

"Ok, I'll try. But it'll cost you a quarter, not no nickel."

"Ok, I'll give you twenty-five cents if you promise that you'll find them. I got it at home. Now hurry Lil' Jim before the bidding starts," she urged, pushing her brother into the crowd that had gathered to watch the bidding. Maggie moved to where the other girls were standing so she could keep an eye on the crowd and maybe catch a glimpse of Johnny Lee.

"Everybody gather around real close and let the bidding begin!" Daddy Robert announced as the crowd grew. The auction was always a highlight of the day even for those that did not have a box or would not be bidding. Every woman there was remembering that special Fourth of July when a handsome young man bought her box and a romance was born. It was always fun to see just who the love bug would bite and all because of a lunch box auction. Daddy Robert held up the first offering. It was a large shoebox that had been covered with red gingham and tied with a big red bow. "Who will start the bidding on this fine box? It sure is heavy. Smells like fried chicken inside and maybe apple pie! Must be a might fine cook that made this box. What am I bid?"

"Fifty cents!" A boy in the back yelled.

"Fifty cents! Now, that's a good start. Who'll give me seventy-five?" Daddy Robert asked. And the bidding went on with the red gingham box selling to Larry Thomas for

$1.85! Nancy Sue Sheppard beamed from ear to ear as she took her box from Daddy Robert and gave it to winning bidder. How lucky can a girl get, she thought.

The next box was not a box at all but a pretty basket with red, white and blue ribbons. It sold very quickly to a tall, skinny boy with red hair. Mary Ann Conner was thrilled to be having lunch with Ray Farmer, even if he was almost two years younger than she was. He was very handsome and besides, her mother was almost three years older than her father.

And so the bidding went. One box after another left the table with the couples going off to sit together on a quilt under a tree and share the good smelling contents. Thank goodness, old Hank Franklin bought Louise Sharpe's box, Maggie thought. And Tommy Joe bid on Sally Queen's basket and won. But that was OK, too, because Johnny Lee was surely out there somewhere waiting on hers. Lil' Jim had told him to not bid until Maggie's came up. This was going to work out just great! "Now, we only have three boxes left. Don't know that I've ever seen one this fancy. Who is going to be the first to bid?" Daddy Robert asked, holding up Maggie's. She could hardly control herself. She didn't know whether to dare to look around the crowd or not.

"One dollar!" A voice shouted from way at the back.

Who was that? Maggie couldn't see. It didn't sound like Johnny Lee but she ought to know that voice.

"One dollar and a dime!" Someone else cried out.

"Two dollars!" The first voice shouted.

"I have two dollars. Now that's a mighty good bid on this box," Daddy Robert said. "Does anybody else want to bid?" Silence. "OK. Then I guess this box is sold to my grandson, Andy! Would the lucky young lady please come forward and claim her lunch box."

Andy! How could Andy bid? Maggie was horrified as she crept toward the bandstand. Eating lunch with your brother! How could he do such a horrible thing! She would never live this down as long as she lived. Where was Johnny Lee Hall? Why didn't he buy her lunch? Where is Lil' Jim? Didn't he tell Johnny Lee to bid? Why in the world would Andy bid on her box? She would be the laughing stock of the town! Red faced, she grabbed the box from her grandfather who looked as surprised as she did and ran toward the back of the crowd. "How could you do such a thing, Andy? How could you bid on my box? You know I wanted to eat with Johnny Lee. How could you embarrass me like this! In front of everybody."

"Maggie…I thought that was Sarah Jane's lunch box. I didn't know it was yours," he stammered. "I don't want to eat lunch with you either. I asked Lil' Jim to find out which one was Sarah Jane's and he pointed this one out. Paid him fifty cents, too. I'll kill that kid when I get my hands on him."

"Well, I paid Lil' Jim a quarter to tell Johnny Lee which one was mine so he could bid on it! I'll bet he thinks he's pulled a funny joke. But the joke will be on him cause I'm gonna' kill him. Eating lunch with my brother! I can just hear it now…'who did you have lunch with on the Fourth of July, Maggie?'" she huffed.

"Well, at least Johnny Lee's not even here. So he won't be having lunch with nobody. But look, Sarah Jane's box just sold to Tim Jackson!" Andy growled. "Come on, we'll go over next to the river where nobody can see us!"

"Where nobody can see us! What do you mean? Everybody already knows. We might as well eat right here in the middle of the bandstand!" Maggie answered as she spread her quilt on the ground and opened the box. "Sit down, brother, we are going to pretend that we are having the time of our life while we decide what we're going to do to Lil' Jim."

And they did just that. Enjoying the wonderful meal that Maggie had so carefully packed into the box. This isn't too bad after all, Maggie thought. Andy's not such a bad guy. At least he doesn't chew with his mouth open or try to make silly jokes. It could be a lot worse.

"Where do you think the Halls are, Andy? They haven't been to church all summer. Even when we pass their house, you hardly ever see them out. And I heard Mama Annie tell Granny Ruth that Mrs. Hall doesn't even come in to buy groceries any more. That the last time she saw her, she looked very pale and would hardly speak."

"I don't know. I just think that Mr. Hall makes his boys work all the time and he doesn't do much but sit around and drink. I think that he whips them a lot, too. I feel real sorry for 'em...but it ain't none of our affair. Mama would tell you not to go stickin' your nose in somebody else's business," Andy answered. "Hurry up and eat so we can go get a good spot and listen to Matt sing. Can you believe that he's gonna' really get up there?"

"I just know that I wouldn't have the nerve to get up there in front of all these people—much less try to sing," Maggie answered trying some of the potato salad. "Andy, what do you know about that Klan bunch? Mary Jane said some feller, that her Pa didn't know, came into their store the other day askin' a lot of questions."

"What kind of questions?"

"Oh, just about the Putnams and stuff. Wanted to know how long Nathaniel had worked for Daddy Robert. What the other storekeepers thought about his workin' somebody that was a criminal and stuff like that."

"Nathaniel ain't no criminal, Maggie. Worked real hard for Pa when we were puttin' out the tobacco and works real hard at the store. Don't cause no trouble as far as I know. Why he hardly speaks to anybody, except Betty. Everybody round here knows Daddy Robert. Knows he's a fair and honest feller. Can't believe that anybody would hold it against him for hiring him. But I do know that there are a lot of people just waitin' for Nathaniel to slip up some way. Watchin' and waitin'. I don't know what they think about him and Betty bein' friendly either. But you know her, ain't never quit talkin'. And it don't matter to who."

"Yeah, I know," his sister answered. "She was certainly asking Mama a lot of questions this morning before we left."

And so the lunch went. Lots of small talk, some laughs, and a few serious moments between the fried chicken and apple pie. Sometimes it's not so bad to eat lunch with your brother or sister.

"WE AIN'T GOIN' TO NO PICNICIN'" on the ground. I've had enough of your lip, Hazel. Now get in there and fix me and the boys some dinner," David Lee ordered his wife as he pushed her through their kitchen door. He had started hitting the bottle early that morning, celebrating 'Independence Day' he had told her, "Every American man got the right."

"Johnny Lee, you and Lem come here. I want you boys to go up to the still and finish fillin' up them jars. Bring 'em down here and put 'em in the back of the truck. There should be at least 30 pint or so. We'll hide 'em in the back of the truck under the straw and then about dark we'll go over and take a look at them fireworks! Make some men might happy and come back with some dollars in our pocket. Y'all be careful now, ya hear! Better not be none broke or spilled. This is mighty good stuff. Won't have no trouble gettin' it sold," he told the boys as he shoved them

out the back door. "Hank, you come here, too. You go up
the creek and don't come back until you got least three
dozen lizards in your pail. There'll be plenty of folk wantin'
to come fish after the fireworks are over and they've
sampled my corn. Gotta have 'em somethin' to fish with.
Them lizards will sell for a nickel a piece and that's clear
money. Now get yourself on up there, boy. You hear me?"
he yelled and gave his son a kick in the seat of the pants to
get him moving. Hazel knew that this was going to be a
long Fourth of July.

NED PUTNAM WAS SLOWLY BEGINNING to relax. He
wasn't sure about Susie. She still stayed close to home.
There had been no other "incidents" and the sheriff had
not been by in more than two months. Nathaniel seemed
to be doing well at Crawford's store even though he really
didn't like it. Oh, the Crawfords were all right but the rest
of the white folks just pretended that he was not there. He
was a little worried that Nathaniel had made "friends" with
the young Crawford girl. He came home almost every day
with some funny thing that she had asked or a story she
told him. At least he had one person besides his parents
that he could speak to and laugh with. He just hoped that it
wouldn't cause a problem.

Ned had told him, "just keep quiet, don't cause no
trouble and they'll come around;" just as the men at the
plant had come around when Ned first begun...come
around to wishin' him a Merry Christmas or Happy New
Year; come around to askin' about Susie when she was
under the weather; come around to not callin' him "boy"—
at least to his face. Yeah, Ned thought, things were almost
back to normal.

He'd convinced Susie to fix them a picnic basket, just as she had always done, and they would take their blanket up on the hill to watch the fireworks and the folks down below as they laughed and enjoyed each other's company. They would be able to hear the music as it drifted up the hill. Almost a part...but not quite. Nathaniel had not been to one of their private Fourth of July celebration since he was a small child. Ned was sure that his son's heart would break to watch the others and not be able to join in...not to be able to bid on the box lunches and share it with the pretty girl that fixed it; not to be able to sit on a blanket and hold her hand as the fireworks lit up the night sky; not to be able to make plans with the other boys to go fishing or swimming. Things that all those below took for granted. But the three of them would enjoy their family party, not dwell on the bad, but be grateful that they at least had each other. Grateful that the white robes had found someone else to trouble and that Nathaniel was safe, at least for now. Grateful that life was returning to normal.

CHAPTER 10

THE PRODICAL SON

"R.L., I NEVER DID FIND MAMA. She's never missed a fourth celebration before. You don't reckon she's sick or something?" Vadie asked her husband as they finished their dinner. "Maybe we'd better ride over to her house and check before the singing starts. She sure doesn't want to miss Matt."

"Yeah. We can go over there," he answered dusting the crumbs off on his shirt. "Maybe she just missed her ride. Didn't you say she's suppose to come with the Hardins?"

"Yes and they're here. I saw them a while ago but I didn't get a chance to ask 'em about Mama," she told him scouring the picnickers for a glimpse of her mother. "Lil' Jim, you and Joe go ask Daddy Robert and Mama Annie if they've seen Granny Ruth."

"When do you reckon they'll be cuttin' them watermelons?" I ask trying to get up without spilling the few bites of coconut cake that were left on my plate. There's nothin better than coconut cake especially with a tall glass of cold milk. I sure don't want to dump what little bit I have left in the dirt 'cause I know there ain't no more. Putting my plate carefully on one corner of the table, "Don't let nobody git this, Mama. I ain't through with it yet. Come on Joe! Hurry up."

"I..I..I'm a comin'. D..d..d..don't be s..s..so bossy!
Y..y..you sound l..l..like Betty," he grumbled wiping his
mouth off on his shirt sleeve.

"Hey, Granny Ruth! Where you been? Mama done
sent me and Joe lookin' fer ya," I called out as I spotted her
comin around the bandstand with a man I ain't never seen
afore. "She and Pa are eatin' over there," I told her pointing
the way.

"Thanks, Lil' Jim. We just got here and filled up our
plate. We'll go over and sit with them if there's a spot,"
Granny Ruth answered with the strange fellow following
her.

"Joe, who's that feller in the red cowboy shirt and
that little string tie like you see in pictures of Grand Ole
Opry fellers?" I ask real low as they followed us back to the
table. "Look, he's even got on boots. Cowboy boots.
Reckon he's a real cowboy? You ever saw him afore?"

"N..n..nope," Joe answered.

"Yeah, there's plenty of room," I called over my
shoulder to Granny Ruth as I hurried back to my cake.

Mama and Pa were talkin' to the Preacher and before
I could tell them that I had done found Granny Ruth, the
stranger said, "Hello, Sis."

Mama turned around on the bench, tilted her head
and kinda stared for a minute like she wasn't sure what she
was seein. "Albert? Is that you Albert?"

"It's me. In the flesh," he told her and a big grin came
across his face. "Been a spell. How you been? How you
been, R.L.?" and stuck his hand out for Pa to shake.

"Been fine, Albert, you?" Pa asked shaking his hand
before letting it go and turning back around to his plate.

"Can you believe it, Vadie? Your big brother's
home!" Granny Ruth said as she sat down at the table.
"Woke up this morning and heard something out on the

porch and there he was...sitting in the swing like he'd never left."

Mama wiped her eyes with her napkin before standing up and putting her arms around the stranger. "Glad you're home," she said with a quiver in her voice. She quickly let him go and sat back down next to her husband. "Sit down and tell us about it. Move over Betty. You and Joe move so he can sit down."

Everybody scooted around to make room. I can't figure this out. I ain't never seen this Albert afore and from the look on Matt, Betty and Joe's face, they ain't either. Granny Ruth sure is beamin' though. It ain't hard to tell that she's glad he's here. But I can't tell about Mama and Pa, they're actin' kinda funny. They're bein' friendly and all but kinda holdin' back.

"Finished a gig over in Knoxville yesterday and thought I'd just come on home before I have to be in Alabama next week. Grabbed a bus to Waynesville and thumbed the rest of the way. Didn't want to wake Mama up when I got here so early, so I just napped on the porch," he said between bites, "Boy, this sure is good. Ain't had food this good since the last time I was home. Now tell me, who are all these folks sitting around this here table starin' at me like I have two heads or something?"

"Why, these are Vadie's children, Albert. Or some of them," Granny Ruth laughed as we all tried hard to find something to do. "If you look real hard at this pretty thing next to me, she looks just like Vadie when she was her age. This is Betty," she began and patted Betty on the head. "Betty, this is your Mama's oldest brother, Albert."

"Pleased to meet ya," Betty said shyly, her faced turning as red as the man's shirt. For once she wasn't full of questions.

"Pleased to meet you, too, Beautiful," he told her with a wink.

"And these are her youngest boys. That's Matt, and Joe, and Lil' Jim," Granny Ruth finished the introductions.

"And mighty fine young men they are," he said as he nodded and looked each one of us in the eye. "Beautiful over there is a Caldwell but these boys are sure Crawfords through and through, R.L."

"They're good boys," was all Pa said as he, too, stared at our newfound uncle.

"Tell us about your work, Albert. And where all you've been. How long has it been? Ten years?" Mama asked.

"Almost. Matt couldn't been much more than four or five and Joe was maybe two, or three. Lil' Jim was just a babe in arms," he answered trying to remember. "Been all over. Been up north some and all the way out to Texas. But most of the time I've been in Nashville."

"You've been to Nashville!" Matt exclaimed, he could hardly believe his ears. "You ever been to the Grand Ole Opry? Or saw Hank Williams or Ernest Tubb or...."

"Whoa, boy," he interrupted. "Not only been there, but played there. Played back-up with some of the best right there on the stage of the Ryman Auditorium."

"Wow!" Matt had truly found a hero.

"Matt sings and picks the guitar, too, Albert. Going to have his public debut this afternoon right there on that bandstand just like you did when you were about his age," Granny Ruth filled him in. "He's getting good at it, too. Why I won't be a bit surprised if he's not on the radio one of these days." The proud grandmother patted Matt's cheek.

"What do you play? The guitar?" Matt excitedly ask. None of us had never known anybody who'd even been to Nashville, much less played at the Ryman.

"No, I tickle the ivories a little bit," he answered to a group of puzzled children. "The piano, I play the piano."

"You gonna' play this afternoon?" Matt hoped.

"Well, I might be able to be talked into it if I can get your mother to sing along with me," he replied looking at Vadie with the now familiar grin.

"No! I'm not singing. That's just for people who sing a lot better than me. I only sing in the church choir where there's a lot of other voices to cover mine up," she quickly retorted.

"Oh, come on now, Vadie. Don't be so modest. Did you fellers know that your mama and I, along with our brother and sister, used to go around to different churches and sing? We were the Caldwell Quartet! People were all the time askin us to sing at church, or weddings or funerals and stuff. Yep, we were somethin'. Really somethin'!"

"Mama, why didn't you ever tell us? Why did you stop? Come on, Mama, sing with Albert this afternoon," we all begged.

"Y'all just hush up. Albert, you've got these children thinking we were something we never were. After Jimmy was killed and Mary Beth got married and moved to Hayesville, singing just didn't seem the right thing to do anymore. Sides that, the others were the ones with the good voices. I just kinda hummed along," Vadie answered wiping a tear.

"Tell us about Jimmy, Mama. Who was Jimmy? And how did he get killed?" Betty wanted to know.

"Jimmy was your uncle, too. He joined the Army in '40 and less than a year later was killed in North Africa. He had a beautiful voice and could really play the guitar. He had a real promising future. Your Aunt Mary Beth and I sang harmony." From the look on her face, I could tell that it had been a long time since Mama had thought about these things and didn't like talking about it now.

"Come on Vadie, it'll be just like old times," Albert begged his sister and looked to Granny Ruth for help. "Tell her, Mama. You can get her to do it."

"It would sound good, Vadie, to be able to hear my children sing again," Granny Ruth volunteered. "But you gotta do what you feel like doing."

"Well, right now, I feel like getting this mess cleaned up so we can go over and get a good spot and listen to Matt," Vadie stated as she began to pick up the dirty dishes. "You boys help me pack everything away and carry it to the truck before they're ready to start. Betty, you go get the quilts out of the truck and find us a good spot where we can see and hear real good."

"Sis, it's good to see you again. I didn't mean to stir anything up. It's just been so long I thought it would be real nice to be like old times again," he told his sister as she finished clearing the table.

"It just took me by surprise, you showing up like this and all. But I'm glad you're here for Mama's sake. She misses you something terrible," she answered before moving away to make sure the children were doing what they were told.

"We need all performers to come around to the back of the bandstand," Daddy Robert yelled into the microphone. "Everybody that wants to sing or play or dance or anything else, come on back here so we can make a list. Everybody else find your spot and settle down. We're gonna' have ourself one more good time this afternoon. We'll be ready to start in about ten minutes."

Mama had brought two quilts and Betty had already found a good spot to spread them out for the kids to sit on. Pa carried one of the benches over from the picnic table for him and Mama and Granny Ruth. He put it behind the quilts where he could sit down and stretch out his long legs.

"You did a good job making Matt's shirt, Mama. He looks real handsome in it," Vadie told her mother when they took their seat. "I hope he remembered to get his new hat out of the front of the truck."

"Mama, tell Joe and Lil' Jim to sit on the other quilt. I'm saving this place for Maggie," Betty ordered. "Y'all move on over. That's your quilt!"

"OK. Let's not argue. There's plenty of room for everybody. Where is Maggie and Andy anyway? Anybody seen them?" Mama asked as she tried to keep her children from making a scene.

"Maggie's probably still looking for Johnny Lee Hall. Guess she's trying to find out why he didn't bid on her box lunch," I couldn't help but laugh as I remembered seeing her face when she found out Andy was the highest bidder. "Here comes Andy now. Bet he won't give me that fifty cents, either," I said under my breath, scooting over to the edge of the quilt.

"What's that Lil' Jim? What did you say about fifty cents?" Mama asked as she made room for her husband.

"Oh, nothing. I just wondered if they would give money to the winners," I lied as Andy gave me an evil eye.

Daddy Robert was back up to the microphone. "Don't know how well this thing is gonna' work. Never have had to use one before but I guess somebody must think I can't yell loud enough anymore for people to hear." The crowd laughed as the microphone roared and crackled. "Now, first off, we have a very special treat in the form of Sam Harkins and his boys. They are gonna' do a little pickin' for us. Come on out here Sam!"

And so it went, one after the other. The Pisgah Mountain Quartet, the Free Will Baptist Church Choir all the way from Waynesville, the Rocky Top Square Dance Team, my friend Harvey's sisters, Sarah Jane and Linda Sue, and so on and so on. Some of them are real good and some of them are real bad. Sometimes it seems like they don't want to quit and Daddy Robert has to go out and tell them it is somebody else's turn. He seems to have to do that a lot when they ain't very good. I am startin' to think that it ain't never gonna' be Matt's turn.

"Now, everybody put your hands together and give a great big welcome to my grandson, Matt Crawford. If you all haven't heard Matt sing, then you're in for a real treat. Come on out here Matt and show these folks just what you can do," the proud grandfather announced as a ripple of polite applause went through the crowd. Pa and Andy whistled real loud and me and Joe hollered for our brother.

Matt looked just as fine as any singer with his new shirt and hat. He acted like he was kinda scared or embarrassed, though, cause he never looked up, just stared at his guitar. As soon as he began to strum his guitar, the crowd quieted down and Matt begin to sing. *"I'm So Lonesome I Could Cry"* never sounded so good...not even on the radio with Hank Williams.

The crowd all stood up and cheered when he finished the last note. Lots of men were whistling, not just Andy and Pa. Some of the girls were screaming. "Sing another one! Sing another one!" somebody yelled from the back.

"That's my brother!" I yelled real loud in case somebody didn't know.

"Yeah! Sing another one!" somebody else called out real loud as Matt just stood on the stage not knowing what to do. He started to walk off when someone yelled, "Don't go! Sing us something else!" and the crowd just kept clapping and cheering. They hadn't done that for any of the rest.

Matt walked back to the front of the stage, cleared his voice, "Thank you all very much. I'll try and sing one more if you really want me to."

"Yeah! Yeah!" the crowd roared.

"*Came in last night at half-past ten, That baby of mine wouldn't let me in...,*" he began and a hush fell over the crowd. He sang two more songs before he finally got off the stage.

"That was my grandson!" Daddy Robert bragged when he finally was able to get back to the microphone and settle everyone down. "Believe Hazelgrove has done and got themselves a star!"

People from every where started comin up to Mama and Pa and Granny Ruth and tellin them how good Matt was and how they knew they must be real proud. Why, a couple of people even slapped me and Joe on the back.

Sam Harkins and his boys came back out and started playin for anybody that wanted to buck dance...and there was a lot. Some could dance real good but some people just looked like they was havin' a fit with their arms and legs goin ever which way. The stage was finally cleared of all the sweaty dancers who could barely catch their breath when somebody pushed the piano up to the front.

"Ladies and Gentlemen! If I can have your attention please," Daddy Robert told the group. "Today we have a very special guest. One of Hazelgrove's own boys who has come home from traveling across the United States and playing before large crowds. Played in Nashville. Played at the Ryman Auditorium. Hazelgrove's own star, Mr. Albert Caldwell! Let's hear it for Albert!!!" and again the crowd went wild. I'm not sure if they know who he is or if they just can't believe that somebody from Hazelgrove has actually been to Nashville. Granny Ruth just keeps wiping her eyes with the corner of her apron and saying, "That's my boy. That's my boy," to anybody within hearing distance.

Albert sat down at the piano and began to play. Now I don't know a lot about piano playin' but I don't think that I've ever heard anybody play the piano as good as he does.

There's Miss Louise who plays for the church choir and then Miss Frances, the sixth grade teacher, plays sometimes when we have programs and stuff at school. But their playin don't sound nothin like this and he don't even have any music to go by. Boy, it sure is something. First Matt singing and now Uncle Albert playin the piano and singing, too.

"Thank you very much ladies and gentlemen. Y'all have been very kind," Albert told the crowd after he had played and sung several songs. "It really is good to be back in Hazelgrove again. Some of you old-timers may remember me and my brother and sisters some years back when we had the Caldwell Quartet." Applause and shouts came from all around. "Well, as many of you know, my brother Jimmy is no longer with us…killed in the war. And my sister Mary Beth done got herself hitched and moved off to Hayesville. But my sister Vadie is still here and I think with your help, we can get her to come up here and sing one song with her big brother. How bout it, Sis, just one…for old time sake?" Albert begged as he flashed his smile to the crowd.

"Let's hear it, Vadie. Come on, Vadie! Sing one with your brother!" was shouted from all corners as applause erupted from everywhere.

"Please, Vadie," Granny Ruth asked as she patted her hand. Finally, Mama stood up and edged her way through the crowd and up on the stage as soft piano music drifted into the air.

"I knew we could talk her into it," Albert bragged as she reached him. "What'll it be, Sis? *I'll Fly Away?*" or "*Will the Circle be Unbroken?*" as he continued to play quietly.

"*I'll Fly Away,*" Vadie whispered and he began to play the familiar hymn. "*Some glad morning when this life is ove'r, I'll fly away….*" they both sang like they had a thousand times before. It was as if the whole crowd was holding it's breath as the beautiful song floated through the air.

When they had finished, no one moved or said a word for what seemed like minutes but it probably was only a few seconds. It seemed like clapping would disturb the wonderful sounds that were still circling through our heads. First Granny Ruth stood up and began to clap very softly and then Pa. Then one by one, the entire audience. No one whistled or hollered out. No one wanted the glorious music that filled our body to be disturbed. Not yet, anyway.

Mama slipped off the back of the stage very quietly. Albert was right behind her. "Come on kids, let's go find your Mama," Pa said stepping across the quilt. We all stood up, no one saying a word, and followed him.

There she was…tears streaming down her face wrapped in her brother's arms. "Oh, R.L.," was all she could manage when she saw us. Pulling away from Uncle Albert, she grabbed Pa's hand and looked at us, her children, standing there, mouths open, not knowing what to say or do.

"Let's go home, Vadie. Let's go on home," Pa told her clearing his throat. "You kids go git the quilts and get in the truck." Still holding her hand, he led her around the bandstand.

I'm not sure why we have to go. Mama and Uncle Albert sang real good. Everybody liked it. It was just beginning to get dark and I'd really like to stay and see the fireworks. But I knew better than to say anything.

"Thanks, little sister. You did real good. Just like old times," he told her as we passed by and squeezed her shoulder.

"Say, Albert, are you gonna' stay a while?" Matt asked his new hero.

"Sure am, Buddy. Wanna stay with me?" he answered.

"Can I, Mama? Can I stay with Uncle Albert? I'll get a ride home soon. Can I stay?" Matt begged.

"Want you home as soon as the fireworks are over, you hear?" she answered looking sternly at her brother. "You'd better look after him, real good."

"Oh, I will. Look after all of them if you'll let 'em stay," he promised. "Send 'em home as soon as the last fireworks are shot."

"Let us stay, Mama. Let us stay, please," Betty piped in. And so it was. Mama and Pa left us with our new Uncle Albert while they went on home.

"Mama, can I talk to you afore we go to bed?" Matt ask. She was sitting in her rocking chair, reading the Bible, when her children rushed into the room. Pa was already snoring loudly in the bedroom.

"Of course you can, Matt. The rest of you go on up stairs," she told us, closing the big book. "Is something wrong? You're not in trouble are you?"

"Oh, no ma'am. It ain't trouble a'tall. It's good stuff. Uncle Albert wants me to go with him when he leaves Sunday. Wants me to go to Alabama and maybe to Nashville and sing and play with him. He says I'm real good and that I can make it big time. Says he can git me connected up with the right people and that I can make records and sing on the radio and everything. I can go, can't I, Mama?" he blurted out.

"What are you talking about, Matt? You're just a child. You have to go back to school in a couple of months. You can't just go traipsing across the country like that," Mama scolded so loud that we could hear every word as we listened at the top of the stairs. "Just because you sang well today and everybody was nice and clapped and hollered don't mean you can just go off and be on the Grand Ole Opry or something."

"I ain't no little boy, Mama. You don't understand. Uncle Albert will send me back by Labor Day and I'll still go to school. But I'll be able to go with him and meet lots of important people and get lots of experience. It's a chance of a life time, Mama. I'll be back by Labor Day...in time to start school, I promise. I gotta go, Mama, I gotta go. I won't never have a chance like this again," he continued to beg.

"You're not going anywhere but to bed, young man. Now I've heard enough of this. Git yourself on up stairs. You'll learn one of these days you can't always believe everything that your Uncle Albert says," she told him as she opened the Bible to let him know the discussion was over.

"I'm goin'," Matt whispered when he had crawled into bed. "Ain't nobody stoppin me either. Albert says I'm good and that he can make me a star. I'm goin'. We're gonna' leave right after church on Sunday. Ain't none of you had better say a word either!" he ordered. "Mama will be proud, you'll see. Proud when I'm a star like Uncle Albert."

"DON'T KNOW WHO YOU THINK YOU ARE Albert Caldwell. Putting such notions in Matt's head," she told her brother as they sat on the swing of their mother's porch. She had gotten up at the regular time this morning but instead of going through her routine of waking her children and fixing breakfast, she had made R.L. drive her to her mother's house to confront her brother. She had made R.L. stay in the truck while she sneaked into the house and woke Albert up and told him to come out to the porch. "You haven't been around in ten years and you just show up and start telling my children all kinds of tales. Puttin' dreams in their head. Tellin Matt that you can make him a star!"

"Whoa now, Sis. Let's start over here," he interrupted wiping the sleep from his eyes. "I think Matt's got real talent and can make it. But he won't ever amount to anything if he stays here in Hazelgrove."

"Amount to something like you?" she almost yelled. "Who do you think you are? Last time you were here was for Jimmy's funeral and you were staggering around drunk. Embarrassed us all. Mama and Pop. They were horrified. Then you didn't even show up two years ago when your own father died! Guess you were just too busy amounting to something."

"I couldn't be here. It wasn't that I didn't want to be. I couldn't."

"And just why not?" she asked not letting it drop.

"I was in prison, Sis. Out in Texas," he reluctantly answered. "Don't look at me like that. I didn't kill nobody or nothin'. It was just a misunderstanding that's all."

"Yeah, well people don't usually go to jail for a misunderstanding."

"Well, this one did," he explained. "I was pretty messed up, drinking and all. I'll admit that. Was having a hard time, down on my luck, when I run into this feller who said he was hiring people to play for some real important people. Some real big-wigs. Was I interested? He'd pay me real good. Well, heck, yeah, I was interested. So I played for two nights. Did real good, too. But when it came time to collect my pay, the feller was no where to be found. Done run off with my money and everybody else's. But I run into him again a couple of months later and collected, if you know what I mean. He charged me with assault and robbery. Judge listened to him and not me so I spent two and a half years locked up."

"Well, you could've let us know? We didn't know where you were? And besides that's your side of the story. Bet the feller you beat up tells another tale."

"I'm telling you straight up, Sis. That's what happened. Mama knows about it. Pop, too, before he died," he confessed. "I wrote them a letter ever month. But you know, Sis, that was probably the best thing that ever happened to me. Got me straighten out. Got me on the right road. Been doin good ever since. Don't drink no more. Travel around and make music, that's all."

"Well, I sure didn't know. Mama never told anybody else. I guess I can understand why you weren't there. But that still doesn't make it right for you to come in here and try to take my child. And that's what he is Albert. Matt's a child. Leave him alone. Don't fill his head with your foolishness. Just because you've always had big dreams and not wanted to live in Hazelgrove and now run into a streak of good luck, don't give you no right…" she ordered again.

"Didn't mean to cause trouble. You got a fine family, Vadie. A real fine family and a good strong husband, too. You're the one who's got a lucky streak. Matt is talented but he's fortunate to have such a good Mama and to live here in Hazelgrove. He'll make it one day. You mark my word. I just thought that I might give him a head start. But he don't need no help from me or anybody like me. He'll make it on his own. Got too much talent to keep it under a bushel. And you won't have to worry no more about me, Little Sister. I won't interfere no more. I promise," giving her a hug. "Don't worry nomore." He kissed her on the cheek before going back inside and closing the door.

"What did he say?" R.L. asked his wife when she got back in the truck.

"Let's get on back home to our children, R.L. I don't think we have to worry any more."

"GRANNY RUTH, WHERE'S ALBERT?" Matt asked as we slid in the pew next to her. "He just runnin late?"

"Why, no, Matt. He's left. Left last night. Got word that he needed to be in Alabama right away so he just packed up and left. I'm sure he's sorry that he didn't get to tell you all good-by," she told the disappointed child.

"But, he told me…. We were suppose to go…." Matt stammered as he darted out of the pew and down the aisle.

"Why is he so upset, Lil' Jim? What's wrong with Matt?" Granny Ruth asked as she watched him run he out the door.

"Oh, it's nothin. Guess he just wanted to tell him good-by or something," I lied.

CHAPTER 11

DREAMS

MATT'S BEEN KINDA SAD ever since Albert left. I heard him talkin' to Mama one night when they thought everybody was asleep. "It's good to have dreams, Matt. There's nothing wrong with that. But it's how you reach for those dreams that's important," she told him.

"I just want to do good, Mama. I love to sing but I don't want to end up here in Hazelgrove just singin' in the choir," he tried to explain to her. "I wanna go places and see things."

"I know you do, Matt. And your Pa and I want that for you, too. We want you to be able to reach for the stars. There's nothing wrong with wanting something so bad you can taste it. What's bad is settling for something you don't want because you're afraid to reach out...you're afraid you might fail," she tried to make him understand.

"But Mama, why did Uncle Albert just leave? Why didn't he at least say good-by?"

"Matt, I guess he was afraid," she told him.

"Afraid? What could he be afraid of? He's not failed. He's traveled all over. Been to Nashville. Even played at the Grand Ole Opry. He's a star, Mama," he said with pride in his voice.

"Well, Matt, ever since Albert was young like you, he's had dreams. Big dreams. Gonna' make it big one day, he'd brag. People would know who he was. When we were singing with the quartet, he always wanted us to do more. Go more places. But that was his dream, not mine or Jimmy's or Mary Beth's. We had other dreams. So Albert just up and left one day. Said he'd show us. Said we'd be sorry. He was gonna' be a star! And he has traveled, played his music for lots of people in lots of places. But he's never really struck it BIG. He stayed away from Hazelgrove for almost ten years because I guess he was afraid that we'd be disappointed in him. Find out he's not the big star that he always wanted to be," Mama explained. "But star or no star, Matt, he's a good person and we'll always love him for just who he is."

"He'll make it one day, Mama. I know he will."

"And you will, too, Matt. Just keep believing and working hard. Dreams do come true. The Lord has given you a gift, son, and He won't take it back. He wants your dreams to come true just as much as you do. But only when the time is right. Now, get yourself on up to bed. We got a good day's work ahead of us tomorrow," she said as she kissed her son.

"But, Mama, how will I know when the time is right? Maybe God will forget to tell me and I'll just go on not knowin' that it's time."

"Oh, He won't forget, son. He's a lot like your Pa. He'll let you know what He expects you to do and when to do it. Now, get on up to bed and don't forget to say your prayers," she answered.

CHAPTER 12

LABOR DAY AND THE COUNTY FAIR

IT HAD BEEN A GOOD SUMMER. There had been a lot of extra work to do in the fields to help Pa out, what with Mort being gone and all. But we had finally found some time to sneak off and go skinny dippin' in the Mease hole after the Fourth of July. Andy, Matt, Joe, Pa and me even spent the night up on Catalooch' River and went fly fishin'. Took a bunch of quilts and slept out under the stars. We caught some trout and cooked 'em right there over a big fire. Pa says that maybe next summer we can stay two or three nights. Boy, I'll bet Harvey or Hank ain't never been campin'.

The apple crop has been pretty good. We all have to help with the pickin' and gettin' 'em ready for market. Pa, Andy and Joe each have a large cloth sack draped over one arm and down their back to place the apples in as they climb the ladder and carefully pick 'em off. My job is to carry the full sacks over to the wagon, empty them out so Mama, Betty and Maggie can shine each one up real nice and place it in a bushel basket. They have to be handled very carefully cause they bruise easy and nobody will buy a bad apple. Pa took baskets full of Red Delicious to the farmer's market at least four times and sold 'em right off.

Mama, Maggie and Betty have been busy putting up beans, corn and other vegetables out of the garden so that we will have them next winter. Mama also has been making some of her Bread 'n Butter pickles for the County Fair. 'Bout every year she wins a Blue Ribbon. A lot of the other ladies just laugh and say, "No use even bringing pickles to the judging, Vadie is sure to win." Mama just laughs, too, and keeps on bringing 'em.

It's a good time of the year. The crops are all about in and put up for winter—except for the tobacco—it don't come in until late in September. Almost all of the apples have all been gathered and taken to market. A big pile of wood is stacked nearby ready for cold weather. Most of the hard work is over until tobacco time. The summer sun is still warm enough for swimming or fishing. Yep, it's a good time of the year.

Labor Day is real special in Hazelgrove and all the surrounding towns. There's a big celebration and county fair that lasts for most of a week, ending on Labor Day, with a big parade though town. Everybody brings their best livestock and samples of the best crops for judging. All the ladies bring jars of pickles, beans and stuff along with all kinds of pies and cakes to be judged. I sure would like to find out how you get to be a judge 'cause you get to taste all that good stuff.

There's plenty of things for the kids to do to...like apple bobbing, catching a greased pig, and climbing a pole. Everybody is there tellin' tales about their summer and wondering what the next school year will be like 'cause it starts the day after Labor Day. All the older kids say the fifth grade is real hard but I just think they are tryin to scare me and Harvey with us bein' the youngest and all.

The parade is a lot of fun to watch. It has clowns, floats, the school band and such. Maggie rode on a float with the Labor Day Queen. I have to admit that she looked real pretty in her long pink dress that Granny Ruth made. It had pink bows everywhere and a matching one held her long blonde hair away from her face. Mama even let her wear a little lipstick.

"No make up, Maggie. You're not to wear make up. But I will let you wear a little lipstick this one time," Mama had told her in order to get her to shut up begging. Everybody says Maggie should have won and that they all know that she will next year.

After the parade, everyone heads for the fairgrounds. The whole family gathers at the Shady Hill Baptist Church tent for hot dogs and sweet tea before going off in all directions to take it all in. Everybody knows that you can get the best hot dogs at the Shady Hill tent but you needed to go to the Elk's Club booth to get a snow cone for desert. "Can I go now, Mama? I promised Harvey I'd meet him over by the game booths."

"Yes, go on now, but don't forget the time and you be back here by three o'clock this afternoon so we can go check on the blue ribbons. You hear me, Lil' Jim?" Mama called as I was already running through the crowd. It was Mama's turn to work in the Shady Hill booth. "Maggie, you've got clothes in the truck, I want you to change before you get something on that new dress," she yelled to Maggie standing under a tree talking to Johnny Lee Hall.

"BOY, MAGGIE, YOU SURE LOOK PRETTY TODAY. You shoulda been queen 'cause you sure do look like one. All you need is a crown," Johnny Lee got up enough nerve to tell her while all the time looking down at his bare feet.

"Oh, Johnny Lee, I bet you said that to all the other girls on the float. But I thank ye' for it. Are you going to be at the dancing tonight?" Maggie asked, smoothing down her dress.

"Nope. I gotta get on home. Pa weren't none too keen on letting me and Hank and Lem come to the parade. But Mama talked him into it. Said we had better get on home, though, soon as it's over. Guess he's got work for us to do." Johnny Lee stammered, wanting to take hold of her hand but knowing better.

"Well, guess I'll just have to see you tomorrow at school. Can you believe we'll be in the eleventh grade? You will be there, won't you?" Maggie purred.

"Don't know. My Pa says I'm too big to go to school. Needs me at home to help out. Mama tries to tell him that I won't never amount to nothin' if I don't go but he just says schoolin' is a waste of time when your as big as me. Says he didn't finish school and he's done alright. Sure would like to come back, though. I kinda like school and learnin'," he confessed.

Maggie didn't hardly know how to respond. Johnny Lee was a good student. Never caused the teachers any trouble and he was always fun to be around even though he never said very much. As a matter of fact, this was probably the most sentences that she had ever heard him put together at one time. "Well, I just know that you can get him to change his mind. And most of the harvest will be in soon, so maybe if you don't get to start back tomorrow with the rest of us, you can come later. I really...hope...so," she managed to stammer as she slipped her hand into his.

He turned the color of her dress all the way down to his toes as he squeezed her hand and quickly let it go. "I gotta go now and find Lem and Hank. See you around, Maggie." He turned and was lost in the crowd.

Maggie watched his dark bobbing head as far as she could. He just had to come back to school. He was one of the brightest students at Hazelgrove High School. Why he could figure math problems in his head faster than anyone else could do them on paper. He just had to come back. Maybe if her Pa could talk to his Pa, he could make him understand how important it was. Yes, that's what she would do. She would talk to Pa and get him to go see Mr. Hall and tell him that Johnny Lee needed to be in school. Yes, she felt much better now that she had a plan.

"Howdy, Miz Maggie," Nathaniel stammered as Maggie turned around and almost ran into him.

"Howdy, yourself," she answered not knowing quite what to say but trying to be polite. "You enjoying the fair?"

"Yes, ma'am. My first." He answered before tipping his hat and walking away.

"Now just where did he come from?" Maggie thought as she watched him make his way through the crowd. People would kinda step aside to let him pass like he had some sort of bad disease or something...or else the men would hold their ground and make him swing way wide. Must be hard being like him and not having any friends or anybody to talk to, except Betty. Can't imagine what they could have in common but Betty seemed to make friends with anybody. Everybody knew she could talk a blue streak.

It sure did make her feel uneasy with him standing there, almost touching her. Like, maybe, he'd been following her or something. She sure didn't want anybody to see her talking to him and starting rumors or anything, especially after what she had heard about what happened in Charlotte. And then after he moved back to Hazelgrove. Maggie quickly looked around to make sure that no one had seen—even if there was nothing to see—people still liked to talk and make up tales. She would just have to be more careful, keep her eyes open, and make sure that she didn't give anybody reason to gossip. And she really should talk to Betty and tell her to watch out and not be so friendly. People might start watching and misunderstand her intentions.

But people were already watching. And listening.

"LOOK EVERYBODY! Look at what I won!" Betty exclaimed as she ran toward the group where me, Harvey, and a bunch of other kids had gathered around to work out a plan of what to do next. "Won it playing BINGO over under the big tent. I'm sure it's pure gold." As she pranced around showing everybody the shinny gold heart locket around her neck. "Look, it even opens up so you can put a picture in it," as she went from one to the next.

All the girls were very impressed and said they wished they had been able to win such a wonderful prize. "That's real nice, Betty. Are they gonna' give away any more good prizes?" Susie asked as she looked the necklace over very carefully, wishing she had gone straight to the BINGO booth. "Well, I know where I'm going next. I'm going to play BINGO! Come on Sara, you too, Nancy. Let's go win us a prize."

"Whose picture you gonna' put in it?" Harvey teased. "Lem Hall?"

"It ain't none of your business, Harvey, whose picture I'm gonna' put in it. But you can be sure it won't be yourn!" Betty snapped as she walked away looking for someone else to brag to. "Hey, Nathaniel," she called to the young man leaning against the wall and watching the crowd. "Look what I just won!" she called again and ran toward him, trying to ignore Lil' Jim and his friend.

"Betty ain't got no boyfriend, Betty ain't got no boy friend!" Harvey chanted after her.

"Hush up Harvey, let's me and you go try to win us some stuff," I said and started moving toward the games. The group separated, as they all wanted to find out just what was going on and where the best prizes were. Harvey and I went to the greased pole climb to check it out. Already several boys and girls had tried to climb up to the top of the 15-foot pole to claim the dollar bill that was fastened there. No one had made it very far because of the lard that had been heavily smeared all around the pole, all the way to the top.

"Come on, Lil' Jim, let's me and you try." Harvey said as he pulled Jim toward the waiting line. "Come on! There's already three people ahead of us."

"You go ahead and get in line, Harvey. I'm gonna' wait until some more people try and rub off some of that lard," I said, laying out my plan.

"Yeah, that's a good idea. I'll wait, too. But how will we know when we've waited long enough, Lil' Jim? What if somebody skinnies up that pole and reaches it afore us?"

"Well, we'll just have to take that chance. We'll stand here and watch until somebody gets most of the way up, then we'll know it's time." I answered circling the pole, looking at it from all angles, measuring where the most lard was and where it had been wiped clean by a climber's clothes. Shore would like to win that dollar cause it'd buy a lot of cotton candy and peanuts at the fair. It sure would be better that winnin' a old gold necklace, that's for sure.

Two kids tried but didn't make it even half way to the top. Bobby Joe Young was the next to try. He rubbed dirt and sand on his already dirty clothes and hands.

"Move back everybody. I need room." He announced in his most important voice. Moving back about five feet from the bottom of the pole, he reached down, rubbed his bare feet and hands in the sand once again, and ran toward the pole, jumping as high as he could to get a good start.

He wrapped both legs around it as he reached up with one hand and then another and began pulling himself up, inch by inch.

The crowd began screaming, "Go, Bobby Joe! You're gonna' make it!" as he inched closer to the top. Only two more feet and he could grab that dollar. "Go, Bobby Joe!" The crowd yelled as it grew larger. "One more foot, you only have one more foot to go!"

"Lil' Jim, I think he is gonna' make it. We've waited too long, Lil' Jim." Harvey whispered in Lil' Joe's ear. "He's gonna' get the dollar."

"That's OK, Harvey, we'll try to catch us a greased pig," I answered as we watched Bobby Joe wrap around the pole and slowly inch toward the prize. In my heart, I hoped that Bobby Joe would claim that dollar, what with his family bein' so poor and all.

The Youngs lived on the main road just before you turn into our driveway. Their house is all dirty and you can't tell what color it's suppose to be cause all the paint's wore off. It smells real bad when you just pass on the road, I can imagine what it like when you get close up. Guess it's because of all the pigs they've got. They must have 10 or 11 young uns. Bobby Joe's in my grade and there's a passel older and a bunch younger. Seems like Miz Young's always got one her hip.

"Ye ow!" Bobby Joe screamed as he reached his right hand toward the prize but could only barely touch the corner that was hanging down. "Ow! OW!" he screamed louder as he swatted something with his hand and began slipping back down the pole. He tried to hang on but with every swipe, he slid a little bit farther down the pole until he couldn't hang on any longer. Falling in a heap in the dirt, he straightened up and tried to get himself together. His pride would not allow him to show any kind of emotion, even though he wanted to cry, cuss, and scream.

He just got to his feet, wiped the new dirt from his clothes and announced, "Yeller Jackets!" before he walked away with his right ear already beginning to swell to twice the size and turning red with the sting.

"Now you can try, Lil' Jim. Now you can try. You're next, Lil' Jim, you're next!" Harvey shouted to the crowd and pushed his friend forward.

There was nothing that Lil' Jim could do, except climb the pole. Bobby Joe had done a real good job of cleaning off most of the lard not only as he inched up but as he desperately tried to hang on sliding back down.

"You can do it, Lil' Jim! You can do it. Grab that dollar!" everyone shouted as I began to climb. Just like Bobby Joe, I put first my right and then my left hand as far up the pole as I could reach before pulling my legs up to my stomach as far as they would come. Again and again, I inched my way up the now not so greased pole. Just as I reached the top where I could grab the prize, everyone began to shout again, "Lil' Jim's done it! Lil' Jim's done it!" Stuffing the dollar in my back pocket, I slid carefully back down to lots of shouts and backslapping.

"Way to go, Lil' Jim! Way to go! Lil' Jim's the best pole climber in these parts!" But I knew better and it made claiming the prize kinda' sad. It wasn't near as much fun as I thought it would be.

"Boy, Lil' Jim, what are you gonna' spend all that money on?" Harvey asked as we moved away from the pole climb to try to find another game.

"Oh, I don't know, Harvey. Don't really feel like I won it fair and square," I answered.

"Fair and square! How can you say that? You were the first one to grab it, weren't you?" Harvey asked, not understanding what his friend could possibly mean.

"Yeah, I guess so. But Bobby Joe shoulda' got it. He was right there until he got stung. And he took all the lard off the pole so it was really easy for me to climb."

"Well, I don't know about that. But you got yourself a whole dollar and if I was you I would buy a bunch of stuff with it," Harvey prompted, hoping that Lil' Jim would find it in his heart to spend just a little of it on his best friend.

"Boy, this is the best cotton candy I've ever had. Thanks Lil' Jim for buying it for me. I'll buy you something as soon as I win a prize." Harvey said as he pinched a hunk of the pink, fluffy stuff off and poked it in his mouth to melt. "Yep, I'm gonna' win and get us some more of this. Ain't this this best stuff you've ever tasted?"

"Gotta go meet my folks, Harvey. We've got to go over to the big shed to see if Mama's pickles won a blue ribbon again this year. I'll be seein' ya," I told my friend and moved away toward the meeting place. But Harvey was already running toward the Stephenson brothers to find out what they were up to.

I had just about finished the cotton candy and was licking the sticky off my fingers when I ran smack dab into Bobby Joe. The paper cone with its little bit of goo dropped in the dirt.

"Gosh, I'm sorry, Lil' Jim. Didn't mean to bump into ya like that," Bobby Joe apologized looking down at the ruined sweet stuff.

"Oh, that's OK, Bobby Joe. I was most through anyhow. How's your ear? Still hurt?" I asked trying to change the subject.

"Oh, it only hurt for a little bit. My Pa put some 'backy on it and it's a lot better now. Heard you won that pole climb," Bobby Joe answered still looking down at the wonderful pink fluff and kicking the dirt with his bare feet.

"Listen, Bobby Joe, I couldn't have made it without you wiping off most of that lard. Sides that, you really shoulda won. You were right there. So the way I figure it, we oughta share the prize. I done spent half of it on two cotton candy cones but here is fifty cents for your share." I said pulling the money out of my pocket and handing it toward Bobby Joe.

"I can't take your prize money. You won it I didn't," he answered not taking his eyes off the two shiny coins in my hand.

"Well, I don't think that I won it fair and square and I don't think I woulda won at all if you hadn't cleaned that pole. So here! This part is yourn," I countered and placed the money in his grubby hand.

"Thank ye', Lil' Jim. Nobody else woulda saw it that way. Hope I can return the favor one day," Bobby Joe said as he moved away, jiggling the money in his pocket.

"Where have you been, Lil' Jim?" Mama asked as I reached the meeting place. "You're late. We were about to leave without you."

"Oh, I just ran into Bobby Joe Young and was telling him I was sorry he got stung," I answered as the family began moving toward the awards program.

"Matt and Joe told us about Bobby Joe. He OK? They also said that you won the dollar at the pole climb. That's really great. You always were a good climber. What are you going to do with all that money?" Pa asked rubbing the top of my head.

"Already spent it," I had to confess. "Bought some cotton candy and stuff. Betty won a real gold necklace. Have you seen it?" Trying to change the subject.

"Yes, we've all seen it. Sure is pretty. But don't you think you should have saved at least part of that dollar? Money is mighty hard to come by and you might need it for something important one day," Pa stated, not letting me off the hook.

"Yes, sir, you're right. I probably shoulda saved part of it. But I did spend it on something important," I answered, not going any further, and skipping on ahead so I wouldn't have to answer any more questions.

Pa and Mama just looked at each other wondering what in the world could be so important at the fair to spend a whole dollar on. "We'll have to sit him down when we get home and get to the bottom of this." I overheard my Mama say.

"Pa, I need to talk to you about something real important," Maggie said as she caught up with her father. "I need to ask you something, and you can't go and tell nobody. OK?"

"Well, sure, Maggie. But can't it wait? We've got to go in here and check on Mama's Blue Ribbon, now," He answered, with a puzzled look on his face. All his children suddenly had important things come up.

"Well, I guess it can wait but not for long. I really need you to do something for me today, Pa. And it's real important," She answered not really wanting to let him get away and then saying he didn't have the time. He just had to talk to Mr. Hall, TODAY! It wasn't right for Johnny Lee to have to miss even one day of school.

"I promise, we'll talk as soon as they award the ribbons, Maggie. You stay close and we'll talk then," he said as they took their seats in the grandstands. "Now, Vadie, I don't want you to go and get all huffed up if your pickles don't win this year, now, ye hear. You can't expect to win every time," he told his wife even though everybody knew it would be just like it had been for the last nine years, Vadie Crawford—Blue Ribbon Winner—1949 County Fair—for her Bread 'n Butter Pickles.

Daddy Robert was up on the stage with Blue, Red and White Ribbons filling the tables behind him. Most of the fair crowd had filed into the stands and filled the seats.

Those who were a little late had to stand at the back. It was always important to see who would take home the prizes and bragging rights for another year. Someone hit a tin bucket with a stick several times as they tried to get everyone to get quiet in order for the program to start. "Let me have your attention, Ladies and Gentlemen! Let me have your attention, please! We need everyone to get quiet so we can take care of business and give these here ribbons out. Then we can go out and enjoy the rest of the day," Daddy Robert yelled as the last few on-lookers managed to find a spot to see. Someone hit the bucket a couple more times for good measure.

Daddy Robert was a big man, over six-foot and must weight two-fifty. He stood up front in his best Liberty overalls, the only brand he would wear, with his long-sleeve white shirt and a red hankie in his back pocket. He stuffed his big pocket watch back in it's place with it's long gold chain draping across his chest. He always had three or four fresh sharpened pencils stuck in his bib pocket.

"You can't never tell when you're gonna' need one, boy. And you always gotta have an extra one sharp if your a good business man," he told me one day when I asked about 'em.

"Now, you all know that I don't judge—don't judge any of the contests. I just announce the winners. Guess that's 'cause I got the biggest mouth," he said with a broad smile while everybody snickered under their breath, knowing he was probably right. "No, this year, we got us some fine judges. Qualified judges. Judges that know what they're doing. Know a good pie or cake or winning cabbage when they see one. So there can be no doubt that the winners are the winners."

"So, let's get started. First with the fruit pies. We had eleven entries this year and they were all real fine. We had apple, blackberry, cherry and one peach. Matt Lofton, was the head judge and he told me it was real hard this year—so hard that they had to go back and have a seconds of most of 'em." The audience laughed and gave one another a knowing poke as Daddy Robert turned to pick up the winning ribbons. Matt Lofton stood over to one side waving at the crowd and rubbing his round belly.

"The White Ribbon goes to Miss Thelma Lou Smith for her apple pie. Come on down Thelma Lou. Didn't you win a ribbon last year?" He asked as she shyly stepped on the stage to receive her prize.

"Thank you, Robert. I did." Was all that she could manage to get out before backing up and getting off the stage as fast as she could while polite applause filled the air.

"Now then, the Red Ribbon will go to Mrs. Mabel Jarvis and her blackberry pie. Can you make it up here, Mabel? Or do you want me to have one of these young 'uns to bring it to your seat?" Daddy Robert asked.

Mrs. Jarvis got to her feet with the help of her husband and a cane. "You know I can make it up there, Robert. It might take me a minute or two longer than some, but I'll get there," she answered indigently to wild applause and cheering. Accepting her prize, she swatted Daddy Robert on the leg with her cane and turned to the audience waving the ribbon above her head. Anyone who was there for the first time might have thought it was the Baseball World Series or something just as important that was going on right there in the middle of that Bandstand. Everybody cheered and there were several whistles as Mrs. Jarvis hobbled back to her seat still waving the ribbon.

"All right, I reckon we're ready to award the Blue Ribbon. Matt said that he had been judging this here pie contest for the last twelve years and that he had never tasted anything as good as Dorothy Peters' Apple Crumb Pie. Come on up here Dorothy. You done won yourself a Blue Ribbon." Daddy Robert announced over the roar.

Dorothy Peters was a very small lady, bent at the waist, causing her apron to almost touch the ground. Her white hair was always pulled up on top of her head in a tiny bun. She never had an unkind word to say about anyone and thus was the favorite of almost everyone in Hazelgrove. She walked everywhere she went, taking canned goods or fresh baked goodies to those in need—just handing it through the door and turning immediately to leave. Her husband had died in a freak accident when they had only been married a few months and even though she had been a real beauty in her day, had never remarried. So she had spent the last fifty plus years in a small, white house, near town; taking in laundry and mending to pay her bills. Yes, this was a very favorite winner and it took Daddy Robert almost five minutes to get the crowd to settle back down so the remainder of the ribbons could be awarded.

So it went. After the pies, the cake winners were announced, and then the different vegetables—tomatoes, beans, carrots, etc. It seemed to go on for hours before finally it came time for the canned goods. First the canned beans, corn and beets. Then came the jams and jellies.

BY THIS TIME, VADIE WAS SITTING on the edge of her seat, trying not to look worried or anxious, but the family all knew that she would be devastated if her pickles didn't even place. It was the only pat-on-the-back that she got every year. R.L. rarely told her that he loved her and only then in the darkness of their bedroom. She was proud of her children, even if Mort had broken her heart by joining the army before finishing his schooling. But she had made up her mind, she would smile, and when the program was over be sure to seek out all the winners and congratulate them. Winning nine times in a row was more than anyone else had ever done—she would just have to be proud of that and would save her tears until she got home to the privacy of her room.

"OK, NOW WE ARE READY for this year's pickle winners to be announced. The third place winner, and receiving the white ribbon for her Bread 'n Butter Pickles is Rose Young." Daddy Robert called out. "Come on up here, Rose, I believe that this is the first time you've ever entered." But no one came forward. "Rose Young. Rose Young are you here? Come on up and claim your prize." He urged again. But still no one moved. "Well, guess that Rose just couldn't make it. Vadie, how about you and R.L. taking this by her place on your way home. You have to pass right by there, don't you?"

"We'll be glad to deliver it." R.L. answered going forward to accept Rose's ribbon.

"Now, for second place. This year's Red Ribbon goes to Hazel Hall for her Sweet Dill Pickles! Come on up here Hazel! Come up and get your prize." Daddy Robert said as he looked around the room.

"Hazel ain't here! I'll claim it!" David Lee Hall yelled out from the back of the room as he began to stagger forward. "Ought to be more than just a little old ribbon. Ought to be a money prize!" he slurred as he grabbed the ribbon from Daddy Robert's hand. No one clapped. No one moved. It seemed that the entire audience was holding their breath. There had never been such a display at the awards program. No wonder that Hazel never showed her face in town any more. As soon as he had staggered outside, the entire group began to whisper to one another about what they had just witnessed.

"Well, we gotta get on with it. We still have another winner to announce." Daddy Robert roared trying to get control once more. "We have the Blue Ribbon for Pickles to award next. Everybody be quite now so I can call out the name." The crowd began to settle down, but whispers of unbelief were still circling the room. "Well, I'll be. If my daughter-in-law ain't done it again! How many times does this make Vadie? We may have to draw a line and say you can't enter the pickle contest no more so somebody else gets a chance. Come on up here, Vadie, and get this here Blue Ribbon!"

Vadie was almost embarrassed to accept the prize. She left her seat and went only to the corner of the bandstand not daring to step on the stage. After the last winner, it almost seemed ridiculous to win. David Lee Hall had spoiled the whole ceremony for everyone. She could hear applause, even got several 'Atta girls' as she made her way back to her seat. R.L. might not show his love for her in public but at least he would never embarrass her or the family. He really deserved this Blue Ribbon for being such a good husband and father and tonight she would find a way to tell him just that. It was really difficult to imagine what kind of life Hazel Hall was living. Vadie vowed to herself to stop by and see her next week. Maybe if she just had another woman to talk to it would make things easier.

R.L. patted her knee. "I knew that you'd do it. Never had a doubt." he told her as he beamed with pride.

"Vadie, why don't you run this ribbon up to the door and give it to Rose. Me and the kids will be waitin' here in the truck." R.L. suggested as he pulled up in the Young's yard that was nothing but dirt with a limp blade of grass here and there. The back of their truck was filled with very tired Crawfords who had had a wonderful Labor Day.

"Ok. I'll just be a minute. We gotta get these children home and in the bed. Tomorrow's a big day and it's getting late." She answered sliding out of the front seat. The Young's house was always run down. Guess with so many young 'uns to feed, there was never any money left over to fix it up or make necessary repairs. Even in the semi-darkness you could tell that several windows were broken out.

Rose must have heard the truck stop because before Vadie could reach the front steps she stepped out through the front door and onto the porch. Two bare-foot, dirty children were clinging to her legs and she held another on her hip. "Evenin' Vadie. What brings you by?" She asked before Vadie could get a word out.

"Evenin' Rose. You weren't at the Awards Program this afternoon at the fair to get your prize, so we just wanted to drop off your Ribbon. You won third place in the pickle contest. Congratulations!" Vadie replied trying not to notice all the unkept children looking out of every window. "Wish you could have been there to accept it yourself."

"Thank ye for bringin' it. Didn't get my dress washed up." She stammered, wipping her hands on her dirty apron before daring to reach for the unbelievable prize. "Didn't have no idee I'd win or I coulda had one of my young 'uns git it." Still shaking her head in disbelief and not taking her eyes off the ribbon.

"Well, we were only too happy to bring it by. It was right on our way. Congratulations, again!" Vadie said as she turned to leave, embarrassed and wanting to run to the truck.

"Wait a minute, Vadie. I forgot my manners what with winning this here ribbon and all. Tell Lil' Jim 'Thank ye' for sharing that pole climbing prize with my Bobby Joe. That's real nice of him," Rose said with a tight grip on the white ribbon while shooing her brood back into the house.

Vadie turned slowly toward the truck not in as big a hurry as before. Had she heard right? Was that what Lil' Jim meant by spending his prize on something important? Guess this was just about the best Labor Day that she had ever had.

"What did she say, Vadie? What did Rose say?" R.L. asked as she slowly closed the door of the truck and looked back toward the Young's house.

"I'll tell you later, R.L." was all that she could manage with the tears streaming down her face. She sure was glad it was dark.

CHAPTER 13

THE NOTE

DADDY ROBERT TOLD ME TO TELL MY PA that he needed for him to come down to the store. "Now, don't forget, Lil' Jim. Tell him it's important."

So after supper, when the kitchen was cleaned and we were all listening to the radio, Pa kissed Mama on the cheek and said he's goin' to see Daddy Robert. Don't know what could be so important that he had to miss the Grand Old Opry.

"Let's go out back, son. I don't want your Mama to see us talking," Daddy Robert told R.L. as he locked the front door of the store. Once they were settled on the steps and Daddy Robert was sure no one was about, he handed his son an envelope. "Read it. Found it stuck under the front door this morning when I came to open up."

The white envelope, dirty around the edges, just had the word "Crawford" scrawled in large letters across the front. When R.L. unfolded the paper inside, it was the same dirty paper and handwriting, almost like that of a child.

CRAWFORD,

LET THIS BE WARNING TO YOU
AND YOURS. FOLKS ROUND HERE
DON'T TAKE KINDLY TO YOUR
KEEPING THAT COLORED BOY.
DON'T LIKE HIM MESSIN
AROUND WITH YOUR
GRANDDAUGHTER EITHER. SHE
SHOULD BE TAUGHT BETTER.
UNLESS YOU SEND HIM ON HIS
WAY, DON'T KNOW WHAT
MIGHT HAPPEN.

CONCERNED CITIZENS OF
HAZELGROVE

R.L. read the note, turned it over, looked at the envelope, and read the note again, certain that he had missed something—that it didn't say what he read. "Who do you think sent it?"

"Don't have any idea. Don't think it actually is somebody that lives in Hazelgrove. Gotta be somebody from the outside, Klan maybe." Daddy Robert answered in a low voice.

R.L. read it again hoping that something would change, that the words would be different. "Have you showed it to the sheriff?"

"No, thought I'd let you look at it first."

"You scared?" R.L. asked his father.

"Not for me. But Mama Annie, you, Vadie, and the kids might be in danger. Especially Betty. She ain't nothing' but a little girl who is color blind and tryin' to do what the Lord would want her to do. Be kind to another."

R.L. could tell by his voice that he was very worried. "What do you reckon we ought to do?"

"Reckon we'll have to talk to the sheriff. See if he's noticed any strange happenings around. See if the Putnams have had any more trouble. After that, I don't know. You don't think that somebody would harm one of the kids, do you?" he needed reassurance from his son.

"Naw, I think they are a bunch of sneaks. Not man enough to stand up and say what they think. We might ought to keep an eye out, especially around the kids. But I think you are right about talkin' to the sheriff. Haven't heard anything, but you know, maybe he's keeping stuff close to the vest. Why don't you give him a call and see if he'll come on over?"

As Daddy Robert made his way back into the store, R.L. couldn't help but look around. Who might be hiding in the trees between the store and house? Could somebody be laying in the tall grass down next to the railroad track, watching?

He didn't want to be alarmed, but he sure didn't want his family in danger. This just wasn't something that happened in Hazelgrove. These were decent, hard-working, God-fearing people that he had known all of his life. He couldn't imagine that any of them would be behind this.

After Sheriff Taylor came and reassured them that he would keep an eye out for any strange happenings and make a point of driving by the store and house several times per day, they were still not comforted. No, he had not spoken to Ned Putnam lately but he would. And, no, he hadn't heard anything about any Klan activity. He was sure that last winter's "incident" was just that, a one time incident and they were gone. This note was just probably some hot-head, letting off steam, but just the same, he urged them both to keep their eyes open for anything suspicious.

After the sheriff left, R.L. and his father just sat on the back steps, quiet, trying not to let their imagination run away with them. Concerned more for the other than for their own self. Concerned for the rest of their family who could not be told because they would not understand and only be afraid. It was their job to protect. That's what fathers do. But how, when you don't know what to protect them from? Would Vadie and Mama Annie notice the fear on their face? Notice the catch in their voice when they tried to assure them that nothing was wrong?

Life could not be lived all huddled in a corner not knowing who could be trusted. No, they were proud mountain men who would stand and fight—if they just knew who they were fighting.

"I'll let Nathaniel go tomorrow." Daddy Robert finally interrupted the silence. "I believe that he's a good boy and just got caught up in something that he can't handle. I'll see Ned and explain that I have no choice."

"You sure you want to give in? You don't want to put it off for a spell and see what the sheriff finds out?"

"I feel like a coward, R.L. Bowing down to some low-life that won't show his face. Goes against my grain to give in to somebody that can't even look a man in the eye. Sends a note—a note that's not even signed. But I don't think that we can wait. If something did happen, I don't know what I would do. No, I'll tell Nathaniel tomorrow and I'll ask him to tell Ned to come by the store so we can talk."

"I'm sure that you are right. Maybe these same folks have been sendin' notes or something to Ned, too. Maybe he knows something we don't. You all have known each other a long time." R.L. said the words, almost to himself, because he could tell that his father was lost in his own thoughts and worries. R.L. just couldn't believe that anyone in Hazelgrove would harbor a grudge against his father just for giving Nathaniel a part-time job. Or against Betty, a child looking at the world through a little girl's eyes. But then, he didn't think he would ever see a cross burnin' in his hometown, either. Things changing and not always for the better. These mountains have been a safe harbor for generations of families...a place where everybody knows everybody else; a place where you could work hard and make a decent living; a place where you could raise children to be honest, kind and respectful; and a place where neighbor looked out for neighbor. But now....

NED COULD TELL THAT HIS SON WAS AFRAID that he'd disappointed his father, again. What words could he say to convince him that this was not his fault...Not his fault that he was born colored in a white community; not his fault that some folks would always think that they were second-class; not his fault that he would have to work harder and hold his head higher just because of the color of his skin.

Ned had not told Nathaniel of the notes he had been getting at work. He had not even told Susie. Notes that were left in the seat of his truck or on the windshield. Notes that he no longer read. Just threw away. It had been going on for weeks now. The first, tucked into the seat where he almost didn't see it, was nothing more than an almost child-like drawing of a man hanging from a tree. A week or more later, there was a second, and this time there were words...bone chilling words. Then, they would be there almost everyday until he got into the habit of looking for them. Always in a dirty white envelope, always written in pencil, always signed by "Concerned Citizens of Hazelgrove" and each more scary than the last.

The sheriff was waiting on him this morning when he got to work. "No, everything's been alright," Ned lied. "We ain't seen no trouble since last spring. Yeah, folks been treatin' us right. No, he hadn't got any note. Tell Mr. Crawford that we don't mean to cause him no trouble."

When he got home and Nathaniel told him that he'd been fired, Ned was not surprised. He'd of had to do the same. Robert Crawford was a fair and honest man and it would take a lot for him to cow down and give in. Yes, Ned would go to see him tomorrow after work. He would tell him that he understood, even though he didn't…didn't understand why his family could not just be left in peace.

"I'm sorry, Papa. I didn't mean to bring trouble on you and Mama. I didn't know where else to go. I thought everything would be alright here," Nathaniel apologized. Ned just shook his head. "I'm gonna try and make it right. I can't live like this any more where I'm afraid to speak or even to look folks in the eye and where I feel that somebody's always watching me."

"I know, son. Your Mama and I thought you'd be safe here, too. Thought things would work out. Thought that Charlotte mess would stay in Charlotte," He told his son.

"I've got some friends down near Atlanta. They've got good jobs where they're treated right. Said I could come down there and they'd help me out. Reckon that'd be best," Nathaniel tried to sound positive. "I've got enough to get me a bus ticket and see me through for a few weeks until I can get me one of them jobs. Gonna make something outta myself. Gonna show all these white folks that I'm just as good as them. Why, there's even a college in Atlanta, a collage for colored. Maybe I'll go to school and get me a education. I'm gonna be somebody Papa. I'm gonna be somebody. Make you and Mama proud."

"Oh, Nathaniel," how could he explain, "We are proud. Proud when you came into this world. Proud now. You gotta understand. Ain't nothing about you...just the way it is. There's good folk all over—white and colored. But they's some bad folk, too. Most just don't know no better. Ain't gonna change 'em. Just gotta learn to let it slide off your back, take a step back, and remember who you are. Your Mama's heart will be broke. But she'll understand. Maybe you could give her just a little bit of time to get used to your leavin' and all. Break it to her kinda slow. Don't just up and leave, son."

"I'll give it a little bit. But I don't know how much longer I can stand it. Don't want to cause any more heartache than I've already caused."

Ned could only nod. Afraid to speak. Not knowing what words he could say to ease his son's pain. Nathaniel was a bright boy. He deserved a chance to make something out of himself. Ned only wished it could be in Hazelgrove.

CHAPTER 14

BIG JACK

SCHOOL ALWAYS STARTS THE DAY AFTER Labor Day and this year I'm in the fifth grade, Miz Beck's class. All my brothers and sisters have been in Miz Beck's class, too, since you're assigned a teacher by what letter your last name starts with. Sometimes that's good and sometimes that's bad. If a teacher asks you if you're related to Maggie or maybe Matt or even Betty, well, that's usually good. 'Cause they're real smart and don't cause nobody no trouble. But if they say, "Aren't you Andy Crawford's brother?" you just kinda nod and wonder what kinda trouble he caused.

Betty says the fifth grade's real hard and Miz Beck don't like no slackers. She's not as nice as Miz Frady was last year. Says she knows now and then we all gotta help out at home but we have to work twice as hard when we git back to get caught up. "School is important if you want to get ahead," she says. My Mama would be real mad if I didn't work hard and get promoted.

We'd had a good summer but it's always kinda excitin' to go back to school. Harvey told everybody right off about us goin up on Spivey and Lem getting snake bit and all. Made it sound like we'd all been in a heap a mess if he hadn't knowed just what to do. Reckon that don't matter none, though. Everybody knows Harvey and how he likes to brag.

Hank ain't been comin regular and Miz Beck's done been after him. "Hank, I want you to tell your mother and father to come down here so we can get this straightened out. You're a smart child but you'll never get caught up if you don't come to school everyday. I know they want the best for you and for you to make something out of yourself. The only way to do that is to be in school—every day. You hear me, Hank?"

"Yes, ma'am, I'll tell 'em," I heard him tell her but I ain't seen any of the Halls come yet.

Betty was shore right. Miz Beck don't put up with people talkin and foolin around and such. "We're here to work hard and learn, children. Just like your father puts a seed in the ground, waters it, tends it and watches it grow until it becomes ripe and ready to harvest, that's what we do here in school. We plant a seed in our brain, we read, do arithmetic, and study hard to make it grow so that one day we'll have the knowledge for a better life," she told the class the first day.

Well, I don't know nothin about that. I ain't never heard of no learnin seed and even if there was such a thing, I ain't figured out how'd it get planted in your brain. But I do kinda like Mis Beck cause every mornin after the bell rings and we pledge allegiance and say the Lord's prayer, she reads us a story. It's usually about a far off place like Africa or somethin and she makes it sound real excitin. We got a big, round ball in our room with the world painted on it. It's a globe and Miz Beck always points to where we're goin that day in the story. I like to close my eyes and play like it's me that's doin all them things and goin to all them places.

School had only been going on six weeks when we had to stay home and help Pa. Puttin up tobacco is hard work. About the hardest work there is. Even Betty and Maggie have to work in the field and I sure ain't gonna' let no girl out do me. I don't want Pa to think I am a baby and can't carry my own weight.

Pa don't believe in hirin' extra help, but with Mort gone off we're short handed. Nathaniel helped in the spring but ain't nobody seen him in most a month. Don't work at Daddy Robert's store no more. Don't know why.

So Pa went off huntin' for Big Jack. If we don't get our tobacco hung in the barn, there'll be no tobacco to sell. It's all been cut and hung upside down on poles out in the field to begin turnin but now it's time to hang it in the barn to finish curing.

Me, I was always afraid of Big Jack. He's right scary lookin. Must be 7 feet tall with a long black beard and long hair. Always wears his army clothes, too. Granny Ruth said I ought not be not be scared, he was just a gentle giant who was misunderstood by most. She should know cause he will just show up at her house now and then to help out. She never asks him, but somehow he just knows that there's a job that needs doin and he just does it. He don't take no pay, not in dollars anyway. But she always sends him off with a poke full of vegetables, a cake of cornbread and maybe some biscuits. He lives somewheres up in the mountains in a one-room shack.

Granny Ruth said that before the war, he worked at the plant and had a wife and a youngun on the way. Something happened and his wife took sick and died. Baby died, too. Granny Ruth tried to help 'em. But she couldn't help Big Jack's wife or the baby. Right after that, Big Jack joined the army and went off to war. When he came back, he couldn't stand to live in his house, so he just built him a shack back in the woods, near the top of Pisgah Mountain.

Big Jack don't work, not at a regular job no ways. He just helps people out when they need an extra hand. When you need him, you just tack a note on a tree at the foot of the trail leadin up to his shack. That's just what Pa did and the next morning afore daylight, Big Jack was sittin on our back steps.

Ain't never seen nobody work as hard as he does, not even my Pa. Shucks, he barely stopped to take a drink of the water that Mama brought out to the field. He set off to himself and ate when Mama brought lunch, too. Don't know that I heard him say more than 4 or 5 words all day. We laid the tobacco on the sled and hauled it to the barn. It was so dark, I was afraid our old mule would run into a tree.

"Come on up to the house and sup with us, Big Jack," Pa told him when we had hung the last tobacco stick in the barn for today. But he just shook his head and walked slowly out of the barn and down the road.

Next morning, he was sittin on our back steps again. That's the way it went for a week, until we bout finished.

After we'd all gone to bed Friday night, I heard Mama tell Pa, "These young 'uns have missed enough school. They'll have to work extra hard just to catch up. You'll just have to get Jack to come back next week and help you finish up. Cause they're goin' to school come Monday. You hear me, R. L.?" But Pa just grunted.

Saturday afternoon as we were unhitching Old Sam from the sled, I heard Pa tell Jack, "I'm gonna' send these young 'uns back to school next week. But if you could come back Monday and help out for a couple of days, I'd be mighty beholden," and he handed him some dollars. I don't know how many, but Big Jack took it, put some of it in his army coat pocket and handed the rest back to Pa.

"Reckon that'll be enough," he said and started to walk away. "You mighty right R.L. These young 'uns' gotta get back in school. Gotta make somethin' out of theirself. See ya Monday," and he went off down the road. Mama hurried back to the house and filled a big basket with all kinds of stuff and had me and Joe run down the road to give it to him. He said, "Thank ye."

CHAPTER 15

BACK TO SCHOOL

AND SO WE WENT BACK. It did take some doin' just to catch up what I'd missed. But a lot of other kids had to stay home and help out, too. That's just kinda the way it is when you live on a farm.

But Johnny Lee did not come back. School had been going on for over a month and still there was no sign of him. When Maggie asked me about Hank, I told her that he come now and then but ain't comin' regular and nobody has seen Lem. Maggie had talked to Pa when they got home Labor Day night. But I heard him tell her, "Now Maggie, it ain't none of our business what David Lee Hall sees best for his family. Don't want no man tellin' me how to raise my young 'uns, and I ain't tellin' no man how to raise his. You go pokin' your nose in somebody else's business and you're just as libel to get it cut off." We all knew Pa was right. If anybody said anything, it would probably just make things worse for Johnny Lee and his brothers.

At recess time, Miz Beck said that me and Hank Hall needed to stay inside and do some catch up work. I reckon that's ok if you only have to do it once in a while. Hank don't like it much either, I can tell. But at least maybe I can talk to him and find out about Lem. I ain't seen him all summer—ever since he got snake bit.

"How's Lem doin? Ain't he comin back to school?" I asked as I took my readin' book and slid in the desk next to Hank's.

"Don't know. Pa says he needs him at home after he was laid up and couldn't work this summer," he answered, never taking his eyes off his book.

"How long was he laid up?"

"Don't know, maybe 2—3 weeks. Doc said he coulda lost his foot if Matt hadn't done what he did," he said, still not looking up. "Still limps a little. Did y'all find the treasure?"

"Nah, we didn't go back. Probably not even up there anyways," I told him. "Tell Lem that I'm glad he made it. Hope he gets to come back to school." I only read a few pages because I couldn't stop thinking about Lem and why his Pa was so mad all the time. The bell rang; recess was over.

That afternoon, me and Joe walked to Daddy Robert's store. It had been a whole week since I'd had one of Mama Annie's cookies what with helpin' in the tobacco and all. Mr. Hall was in the back of the store again, talkin to Daddy Robert. He looked real mad. Madder 'n usual. Me and Joe just stayed up front near the front door where we could watch what was goin' on. There wasn't nobody else in the store.

I saw Daddy Robert shakin his head "no" and it seems like Mr. Hall got even madder. "David Lee, I'll give you credit. Hazel can come in anytime and get the groceries or other stuff she needs but I won't give you no money," Daddy Robert told him very firm.

"Hazel won't be needin your groceries, old man. We ain't beggars. Just need a little loan till I git on my feet!" he almost shouted, shaking his fist at my grandpa.

"I'm afraid that what you need the money for won't get you on your feet it will just get you father down in that hole. Your fishing lake would make you a good living, David Lee, if you would just stay away from the bottle and that still of yourn," Daddy Robert said trying to be calm and looking around to see who else might be in the store and listening. He saw me and Joe looking at them. "Now, go tell Hazel and the boys to come and get what they need. You've got a good wife and three fine boys, David Lee; you ought to get yourself straightened up." Daddy Robert walked over to me and Joe as Mr. Hall stomped out the back of the store, slamming the door. "And just what can I do for you two fine young men today? Would you all be lookin for cookies?"

"What's he all mad about, Daddy Robert?" I asked.

"Oh, nothing, that won't be all right once he sobers up, Lil' Jim. Now let's go see if we can't find Mama Annie. Where's Matt and your sisters this afternoon?" he said trying to divert our attention.

"Matt's a playing ball over at the high school gym with Andy and some more boys. Andy says they've got a new basketball coach and that he might just play this year. Maggie had to go by and see Granny Ruth. I think Granny Ruth's makin her a new dress or something. Betty must've gone on home. We'll take them a cookie, though. Boy, that Mr. Hall sure was a sight when you was tryin' to give out the ribbons, Daddy Robert. Why do you think he's so mad all the time?" I asked, not wanting to let the subject drop.

"Well, Lil' Jim, I don't know nothin' about that. Reckon we had just better tend to our business and let the Halls work on theirs." he answered, letting me know that that was all he wanted to hear about David Lee Hall. "Now, Lil' Jim, when was the last time your Mama heard from Mort?"

It sure was hard to figure out if I wanted chocolate chip or peanut butter off the big plate that Daddy Robert pulled out from behind the counter. "It's been at least two weeks, I guess. He's still up in Pennsylvania. Think he still writes Becky Peterson regular. Kinda makes Mama sad that she don't hear much from him, though." I volunteered. "Guess we'll be goin' on now, Daddy Robert. Gotta see if Pa and Big Jack got finished with our tobacco. Tell Mama Annie 'thank ye' for the cookies." Throwing my book sack over my back, Joe and I headed for the door.

"Oh, I've been meaning to ask, how's that little kitten that Nathaniel found and gave to Betty a while back?" Daddy Robert called after us. "She got it back on it's feet?"

"Yep, it's as spry as one thing. Sleeps right in the bed with her and Maggie. Mama says she don't know when we started runnin' a animal hospital. That if Betty don't stop bringin' strays home that there ain't gonna' be any room left in our house for the rest of us." I told him. "See you tomorrow, Daddy Robert."

"Yep, s-s-se you to-to-tomorrow," Joe called. Joe was never one to talk much. Not even to family. Guess I'm about the only one he ever really says things to.

It was one of those real hot days in the fall that kinda feels like it's gonna' be summer all over again. The leaves are turning all colors and beginning to fall. They kinda make a crunchin' sound when you walk on them. Pa says that this is the best time of the year 'cause you can see "the fruits of your labor." Now, I don't rightly know about that. I sure hope Pa and Big Jack are through puttin' up the tobacco 'cause that's a lotta work. I do know that I'm glad all the pickin' is done, and I won't have to do no hoein' for a spell. I don't much like hoein'.

"Come on, Joe. I'll race ya!" I yelled already running.

CHAPTER 16

OCTOBER, 1949—MISSING

"LIL' JIM, WHERE'VE YOU AND JOE BEEN? Didn't I tell y'all to hurry on home this afternoon? Got work to do." Pa shouted as we came into the yard. "Me and Jack worked all day puttin the last of the tobacco in the barn and I needed you boys to carry these here jars. Had to carry 'em myself and put 'em up, too. Put them books on the porch and get yourself out here."

I could tell right off that he was mad and there ain't no use makin excuses. "Sorry, Pa, guess we forgot. We stopped by Daddy Robert's store but we didn't stay but a minute," I told him as we reached the can house.

"Yeah, w-w-w-e just stayed a m..m..minute." Joe stuttered.

Pa had already gone inside and was busy putting jars on the shelves of the little, rock building. There were jars of beans and corn and tomatoes sitting in neat rows on their shelf like they were just waiting for the day that it would be their turn to fill the bellies of the Crawford clan. Then there were the jars of jelly and jam—blackberry, apple, cherry and my favorite, strawberry. "Your Mama's got a lot more ready in the kitchen. You boys go get you a load in that basket and bring 'em down here. Want all these jars put up before supper. But be careful and don't drop any. Your Mama's worked hard puttin this stuff up. Don't want any broke," Pa ordered as he put the another jar on the shelf.

It seemed like there was no end. We carried jars of pickles, pickled beets and chow-chow to the can house for Pa to put on the shelves. Row after row. I didn't know there were that many jars in the whole world.

"You'll be glad to have this good food this winter. You shouldn't complain so much." Mama said when Joe asked her if we could quit. "This is the last load."

"It's a good thing, 'cause there ain't no more room," I said as Maggie wandered into the kitchen. "Yeah, Maggie, you know when to come home. When all the work's done. Mama, make her take a load. She ain't done nothin' to help out."

"Don't tell me I ain't done nothin' to help out! Who do you think helped Mama put all that stuff up this summer? Me! I helped her fill every one of them jars. Tell 'em Mama! Tell 'em I do my part and then some," she ordered as she took a package from under her arm and carefully unfolded the brown paper. "Look Mama! Granny Ruth ordered the material all the way from Asheville and made me this dress to wear to the Harvest Dance next week. Ain't it pretty?" she asked as she held the green and white dress in front of her and twirled around the room like she was dancing.

"I swear, Maggie, Granny Ruth spoils you. All the time making you dresses and such. Why, you've got more clothes now than everybody else in this house put together. Now, go put it up and come down here and help me get supper ready." Mama teased and swatted her on the bottom. "You boys tell your Pa that this is all and supper will be ready shortly. And tell Betty to come on in and get cleaned up." she instructed as we carried the last basket full of jars out the back door.

"Ain't seen Betty, Mama. She ain't been helpin' at the can house." I called back only too glad that this would be the last trip. It was beginning to get dusky dark and it was hard to make your way to the can house where the only light was Pa's lantern hanging on a nail near the door. It seemed like each load was heavier than the last.

"Well, go look in the chicken house. Or see if she's in the barn looking after one of her critters." Mama ordered as she stood in the back door looking toward the barn. "And where is Matt and Andy? Why aren't they home?" she called to no one in particular.

GOING BACK INSIDE, she began to stir the beans on the stove. Where were her children? They all thought they were grown and getting much too big for their britches. She'd just have to have a talk with R.L. and tell him they need to get these boys in line, she thought as she opened the oven to check on the cornbread.

Maggie returned to the hot kitchen. She didn't know how her mother stood it. It was an exceptionally warm day for early October and with the wood cook stove going full blast, the kitchen must be at least 120 degrees. Even with all the windows and doors open, there was still no air stirring through the frame house. Her mother had been a beautiful woman, or at least that what everyone had told her. Maggie really was proud when someone commented that she looked just like her mother. When Vadie had married R.L., she'd had long blonde hair like Maggie's and just a sprinkling of freckles across her up-turned nose. Now, there were a few streaks of gray and the freckles have given way to brown age spots. After seven children, her figure is a little round and plump, but anyone who took hold of her hand would immediately know that she was not a pampered wife. She worked along side of her husband in the fields and still managed to give her family a warm, loving home. No one ever heard Vadie Crawford complain about her lot in life. "I'll set the table, Mama." Maggie said taking the dishes out of the cupboard.

"Have you seen your brothers?...or Betty?" Mama asked still stirring the beans.

"Andy and Matt were playing ball with some other boys at school. Haven't seen Betty. I went to Granny Ruth's right after school and then came on home." Maggie answered placing eight plates around the long table.

"Supper ready?" Matt and Andy's voices echoed from the front porch. "We're starving."

"Now, just where have you two been? It's gettin' late. Just like you two to show up when the work is done." Mama snapped at the two coming into the kitchen. She always wanted to know exactly where her children were and what they were up to. Reckon that was why she got so upset when Mort announced he was goin' off to join the Army. When R.L. or one of the kids would tell her that she worried too much, she would just say, "It's a mother's right. When somebody starts calling you Mama, you'll understand." But she really knew that they probably would never realize how she felt. Maybe it was because she had such a difficult time bringing each one of them into the world. She had been sick for nine months with all seven. Then when the time came for them to be born, it always seemed like they wanted to stay right where they were—in the comfort of her womb. If you looked at each one, though, they had all turned out pretty well. Each so different, yet so much alike. Vadie knew first hand about growing up on a farm surrounded by mountains and people who thought that this was all there was. The folks of Hazelgrove were good, solid people who worked hard, helped their neighbor, and raised their children to be God fearing. But most didn't realize that there was a great big world out there with wonderful opportunities to be snatched. She knew that her children didn't have to grow up and work at the plant or grow tobacco—worrying if there would be enough money to make it through the winter. She wanted more and it was why she pushed them so hard. Even Mort joining the Army would have been OK if he had just waited and finished high school. But sneaking off like that had not given her time to think on it—to prepare herself for one of her brood to be away from the nest. He was just gone. And he rarely wrote, which was difficult to accept. Well, none of her other children would do anything like that. Of that she would make sure. "Go get washed up. Supper's almost ready. Did you boys see Betty on your way home?"

"No, ma'am." Andy answered. "She's probably taking care of one of her animals somewhere. Mama, if me and Matt join the basketball team, will you and Pa come and watch? They got a new coach down at the high school and he says I'm so tall that I should play. Do you think I can, Mama? Do you think Pa will let me play?" He called from the bathroom where he had lathered the soap all the way up to his elbows.

"Let you play what?" Pa barked coming in the back door with Lil' Jim and Joe not far behind. "Won't be nobody playing nothin if you boys don't start doin' your chores around here. Y'all know everybody's got to do their part. Won't have no slackers in this family. Where you boys been?" he grumbled as he made his way to the sink to try to get the day's labor off his hands.

"Ah, Pa," Andy begged, wiping his wet hands on the seat of his pants. "We'll do our part. You'll see. If you'll let us play basketball, we'll do more than our share. Won't we Matt?"

"Yeah, Pa. We'll do what ever you need. The new coach says Andy could be their best player. Says if he works real hard and does good, he might git a scholarship or something. Git to go to college when he graduates in the spring," Matt chimed in. "Says he had another player at his last school that's goin to Carolina this year. Paid for, too, just cause he plays ball. Wouldn't that be something, Mama. Andy goin' to college—free—just to play ball."

"Nobody gets anything free! Matt, you should know that. You gotta work for it. And I imagine that there'd be a lotta work to go to college—not just ball playin," Mama answered as she went to the backdoor. "R.L., have you seen Betty this afternoon? She hasn't been in the house." Mama asked looking into the dim light. "Lil' Jim did you boys look in the chicken house?"

"Yeah. We looked. She ain't there."

R.L. walked past his wife and out onto the back porch, "Betty!" he hollered, "Betty!" as he stepped out into the yard and made his way to the front yard. "Betty!" His voice echoed through the hills.

"Did any of you see her after school?" Mama asked as the worry crept into her voice. "You know Betty doesn't like the dark and always makes sure she is in the house before you have to light a lantern. Maggie, did you see her?"

"I left school and went straight to Granny Ruth's. Then I came on home." Maggie answered, sensing the worry in her mother's voice. "Maybe she stopped at Daddy Robert's and it started getting dark so she's afraid to come on home."

"We didn't see her when we were there, did we Joe?" Lil' Jim volunteered.

"N..n..nope. W..w..we didn't." Joe finally got out.

R.L. came through the door. Worry was etched on his tired face. "Ain't like Betty not to be home when it starts gettin dark. Vadie, you sure she's not at the store or at your Mama's?"

It was extremely difficult for Vadie to keep herself under control. "Maggie was at Granny Ruth's this afternoon and she wasn't there. Lil' Jim and Joe went by the store and they said they didn't see her. If we just had got that telephone, we could call them and find out. What are we going to do R.L.? This is just not like Betty." Her voice trembled and tears streamed down her face.

Maggie tried to comfort her. She put her arms around her waist, giving her a hug. "You know Betty, Mama. She's probably stopped somewhere to help somebody with an animal, Mama. Don't worry. She'll be all right. Why, we'll all laugh when she gets home and gives us all a big story about how a dog or cat woulda died if she hadn't stopped to help out."

"Maggie's right Vadie." Pa said trying to be as sure as he hoped he sounded. "Andy, take the truck and go to the store and ask Daddy Robert and Mama Annie if they've seen her. Then go over to Granny Ruth's and see if she's there." He began to bark orders to cover his fear. "The rest of us will get lanterns and do some looking around here. Vadie, you stay here in case she shows up. You can ring the bell to let us know."

"Oh, R.L., I'm so worried." Mama cried as she wiped her hands on her apron. "If we just had a telephone…."

Andy took the keys off the nail and hurried out the door.

"Now Lil' Jim, you and Joe get a lantern off the back porch and go the barn and then out in the pasture. Maggie, you and Matt get a lantern, too, and walk down the road to the Young's and the Hall's and see if they've seen her. I'm goin' down toward the creek. Vadie, quit your pacin'! She's all right! We'll find her. Then you can give her a piece of your mind for scaring us like this." He tried to take charge and reassure his family but the only thing he could think about was the note that Daddy Robert had gotten. Surely that couldn't have anything to do with this. He had to put it out of his mind.

Each one did as Pa instructed. No one said a word. They were each wrapped up in their own fears, afraid that putting it into words might make the worse come true. Hoping that if no one said anything, it would be all right.

THE LANTERNS GLOWED in the dark. Vadie thought they looked like large fireflies as the dark silhouettes of her family made their way into the night. Kneeling on the rough boards that made up the back porch, she began to pray. She was still praying when they came back to the house. Looking at their anguished faces, each confirming her worst fears. First it was Joe and Lil' Jim, "Didn't see her Mama. We went all the way to the apple orchard and even looked in the tobacco barn. But don't worry. Somebody will find her. She's probably at Granny Ruth's." They both tried to reassure her as they sat down on the porch steps to wait with her.

Next came Matt and Maggie. "The Youngs ain't seen her but said they'd be glad to help look if we needed them." Matt reported.

"Johnny Lee said he'd been home all afternoon and was sure she hadn't passed their house or he'd of seen her." Maggie added. "Andy will probably find her in town."

"You kids go on in the house and get you something to eat." Mama said as she sat down on the top step and stared into the dark. At least the moon was beginning to peek through the clouds. "Maggie, fix the boys some supper."

They went inside but were not hungry. Their appetite would only return with Betty. But Maggie did as she was told and spooned beans into a plate for each of them and placed a slice of cornbread on the side. She poured glasses of milk and sat them at each place. "Say the blessing, Matt. It's your turn." she whispered trying not to cry.

They were all only too glad to bow their heads and close their eyes. For a moment maybe it would all go away. "Lord, we thank ye for this food." He began and after a long pause, continued, "And see that Betty gets home safe. Amen." It was all he could manage.

Moving their food from one side of the plate to the other, no one said a word. They could hear their mother outside softly praying and crying. Then the rattle of Pa's truck broke the silence. Surely Betty was sitting in the seat next to Andy telling him how to drive. Surely he had found her. Found her at Granny Ruth's nursing a hurt cat. Or maybe at Daddy Robert's and Mama Annie's eating a cookie. Surely…they thought as they scrambled to the back door, afraid to venture any further.

The truck lights lit the front porch and then the back before it came to its resting place behind the house. Cutting the motor off and the lights out, Andy was almost afraid to get out with his news. Granny Ruth had insisted on riding back with him and he was thankful for her calming presence. How could he tell his mother that no one in town had seen Betty since school. And no one seem to have a suggestion as to where he might look. So there was nothing more that he could do except make his way back home. He had known when the trucked rounded the curve into the yard, the news at home was not any better than his.

His mother just looked at him with a blank stare. He wasn't sure if she even saw him or Granny Ruth. She just sat on the step, rocking back and forth, her arms wrapped around her knees. He really wasn't sure—he could just barely hear her—was she crying...or praying...or singing?

"Vadie," Granny Ruth softly whispered as she sat down beside her daughter. "It's going to be all right. We're gonna' find her."

CHAPTER 17

FEATHER OF AN ANGEL

I WOKE TO THE SOUNDS OF HUSHED VOICES on the porch and in the kitchen. The morning sun was just beginning to edge into the sky over the fog that hung in the valleys like fallen clouds. It was hard to remember what was goin' on. When had I fallen asleep on Mort's bed in the sitting room? I can still hear Mama's soft cries somewhere in the house. It was the last thing that I remembered as I tried to stay awake last night. Now it seems that there are people every where. I can smell the strong coffee that is brewing in the kitchen and hear the clink of cups that someone is getting out of the cupboard.

"Sheriff, I just don't know where to start lookin'," Pa was saying to somebody on the front porch. I rolled over in the bed and peeked out the window to see who he was talkin' to. "Last night I walked up the creek bank clear to the ridge and circled around back down to the apple orchard. Andy and Matt went around by the barn and up behind the pasture and all way 'round the fence row. I just don't know.... I just keep thinking about that note. You don't reckon..." his voice trailed off.

"We've got plenty of help here, now, R.L. And Joe Henderson's on his way with his dogs. We'll find her. She's probably fallen, maybe got hurt and can't make it home. Can't believe that this has anything to do with Robert's note." The sheriff tried to comfort him. "Now, you know this neck of the woods better than anybody, so what I want you to do is just give us the directions we need to set off in first. I'm gonna' divide these fellers up into groups of four or five apiece and we'll look at every inch of this end of the county if we have to."

"It's just not like Betty to go off and not be home afore dark, Sheriff. Let me get a cup of that coffee that Granny Ruth's makin' in the kitchen and we'll set off," R.L. shook his head and answered.

R.L. HAD BEEN UP ALL NIGHT, walking through the woods, down the stream that wandered around the edge of their property and then across the field and up on the mountain. All the time calling for her, listening for an answer but hearing none. He had only come back to the house three times to fill his lantern with oil and see if somehow, someway she had made it home, only to leave and search again. If he could have thought clearly, he would have been amazed at the number of caring neighbors that had shown up in their yard this morning. Word had passed from one house to another during the night and early morning hours. They walked, drove, or hitched a ride in order to see what they could do to help out. But all he could think about was the note.

"YOU MEN COME ON AROUND BACK and git yourself some coffee to warm your innards. It may be a long day," the sheriff called to the group of fifteen or so men that were milling about in the front yard.

I could barely see 8 or 10 more men in the back yard, talking quietly among themselves and sipping Granny Ruth's coffee. Each one had their own opinion as to what might have happened and just glad that it was not one of their own that had gone missing.

"Now, here's what we're gonna' do," Sheriff Taylor said as the group huddled close. "R.L. and his boys covered most of his property last night. But it was dark. So we're gonna' split up and look again. Seth, I want you to take 3 or 4 and go up the mountain behind the apple orchard. Go all the way up to the top and come back around and down the ridge. Levi, get you 3 or 4 and follow the creek. Look 15 to 20 yards either side. Sam, you take some men and go down the road toward town. Go all the way into town if you have to. She's gotta be out there and we're gonna' find her. Listen for the bell. When someone finds something, send word back to the house to ring the bell."

And, so it went. I listened as the sheriff barked orders, not knowing whether to lie still and hope it would all go away or go out on the porch and find out which group the sheriff wanted me in. I decided on the latter.

"Pa, which way do you want me to go?" I asked, rubbing my eyes hoping that all these men would think that I was just trying to get the sleep out of 'em.

"I need you and Joe to stay here, Lil' Jim. I need you to make sure the women folk have plenty of firewood and I need you to feed the livestock. Maggie's in the barn now doin' the milkin'," Pa answered as he rubbed the top of my head. "If there's news, ring the bell and we'll all know to come in. Can you do that Lil' Jim?"

"I'll do it, Pa." I answered as I watched the men gather their things and form into groups. The fog had started to lift until you could see the barn as it's tin roof tried to grab the morning sun. The red and gold of autumn had begun to turn brown with leaves littering the ground. I always loved this time of the year. The mountains looked almost like they were on fire sometimes when the sun hit them just right. I could only imagine what the night must have been like for Betty—cold, hungry, afraid of the dark. She must be hurt real bad not to have made it home, I thought to myself as I went to the woodshed. She shore was gonna' have some tales to tell when she got home.

Joe was already there loading up his arms with as much kindling as he could carry. I didn't hardly know what to say to him so we just went about our usual chore in silence. I was sure that anybody who was listenin' could hear my heart beatin' for it was about to bust outta my chest. After several loads, the boxes were filled. "Do you want to feed the chickens or go down to the barn and feed the cows, Joe?" I asked hoping that he would say that he would take care of the chickens since that was Betty's job and I just didn't think I could go in the hen house.

"Don't matter none," Joe answered as clear as anyone would talk. There was not a trace of his usual stuttering. After a long pause, he volunteered, "I'll feed the chickens and gather the eggs."

"Suits me," was all that I could manage as I headed toward the barn. The air was crisp but beginning to warm. Only a few wisps of the morning fog remained hanging on to the treetops like giant cotton balls. Our barn is pretty good size for the farms around Hazelgrove. The brown wood is topped off with a shiny silver tin roof and the dirt floor is almost covered with fresh cut hay. Maggie's head was bent down with her cheek resting against June, our youngest cow. Her eyes were closed as she sat on the small stool and pulled the milk.

"I'm gonna' put Old Sam and Mary out in the pasture," I said reaching for the latch on the stall.

Startled, Maggie bumped the milk bucket with her foot almost turning it over. "Don't scare me like that, Lil'

Jim. It's a wonder I didn't spill it all," she scolded and continued with her job. "You can go ahead and put the cows out, too. I'll be finished when I get through here. Don't guess there's any news yet?"

"No. Reckon not." It was as if the animals sensed that something was wrong. They minded better than they ever had, even Old Sam. As the big, wood gate swung back into place and I put the loop of rope around it to fasten it shut, I noticed somebody coming across the pasture. Must just be someone else comin' to help out, I thought. But as he grew closer, I recognized Big Jack and he was carrying something in his arms. Taking long strides, Big Jack covered the distance between the back fence and the barn in short order. "Maggie…come here," I called as I stepped back into the barn doorway not taking my eyes off of Big Jack and his bundle.

Maggie came to the door and we just stood there, looking at the strange sight. Big Jack had something wrapped in a quilt and cradled in his arms. It was as if he did not see us standing there. He pushed the small walking gate open with his left hand, holding the bundle tight with his right and continued walking toward the back of the house. His face was solid and his eyes just stared straight-ahead, never blinking. Maggie and I followed close behind wondering what he could possibly have. When he reached the back porch, he gently laid the quilt on the boards of the floor. Granny Ruth pushed the back door open and looked down at Big Jack and his bundle. No words passed. They just looked at each other. It seemed like ten minutes but must have only been a ten seconds until Granny Ruth realized what he had brought. I will never forget the scream if I live to be a hundred.

Maggie pulled the cord on the bell and it drowned out the cries of everyone at the house as it echoed through the hills and valleys. It rang until I was not sure if she was still pulling the rope or if the ringing was just in my ears. Big Jack sat down on the top step of the porch like I had seen him do many times when he came to help Pa with the chores. His head was bowed almost to his knees and his arms fell by his side. I had never seen him look so tired, not even when he had worked in the tobacco from sun up to sun down.

Granny Ruth finally got control of herself and began to take charge. "Robert, go get Doc Prichard. And bring the preacher, too. We're gonna' need them both." she told him through her tears. "Rose, help me lay little Betty on the bed in the front room. Don't need Vadie seein' her this way. Not until we get her cleaned up. You children go find your Pa. Tell him to git home."

Daddy Robert moved faster than he ever had as he ran to his truck. He cranked it up and slung dirt as high as the roof as he speeded down the road.

It was not until Granny Ruth mentioned Mama's name that I realized she had not come out on the porch with the others. "Granny Ruth, where's Mama?" I whispered before she could go back into the house.

"She's restin', Lil' Jim. Now y'all go find your Pa," she repeated as she carefully picked up one end of the quilt and Miz Phillips the other. Someone held the door as they moved gently into the kitchen and out of sight. Still not saying a word, Big Jack sat on the porch step as if he was frozen.

It didn't take long to find Pa. He had heard the bell and was already running through the pasture toward the house. Everyone in Hazelgrove musta heard the bell because soon the entire yard was filled with the returned searchers. No one seemed to be concerned about the dirt and scratches that covered them from head to toe. They just milled about the yard whispering to one another, afraid of what they were about to learn.

Granny Ruth met Pa just as he stepped onto the porch. She didn't say anything, just bowed her head, but Pa musta knowed 'cause he just eased by her and went in. The sheriff was not far behind and he paused only long enough to ask Granny Ruth something I couldn't hear before going inside.

Sheriff Taylor came out of the house and sat down on the steps next to Big Jack. "What can you tell me, Jack? Where did you find her?" he asked softly.

Big Jack just shook his head, almost afraid that his voice would not work but finally whispered, "Up on the mountain between here and town. Didn't hear til this mornin' R.L.'s girl was missin'. I was comin' from my place to help look when I just come up on her." He never looked up, never took his eyes off the ground in front of his feet.

"Was she wrapped up in that quilt when you found her?"

"Nope. That's my quilt that Miss Ruth made for me," he struggled to answer.

"We'll talk some more later, Jack. I need to be gettin' back inside. You all right?" the sheriff asked, putting his hand on Jack's shoulder.

Jack just nodded, still lookin' at the ground. A few minutes later, he got up and headed through the field toward his house, never sayin' nothing else to nobody.

The day seemed to be a week long. Daddy Robert got back with the preacher and Doc Prichard and they quickly went into the house not stopping to talk to anyone. Other people came and went. They'd stop on the porch and pat one of us on the head before going inside. Some would say, "I'm sorry." but nothin' else like they didn't know what else to say. Me, Matt and Joe just sat on the back steps all day. Afraid to go inside. Afraid to say anything. Afraid to move. Wanting to talk to Mama and Pa but not knowin what to do. We could hear the preacher and Granny Ruth talkin' to Mama but she never said nothing back.

Doc Prichard was talkin' to Pa and the sheriff. Sayin' stuff like, "There's marks on her neck and that she'd been violated." What ever that means. Pa said stuff like, "I'll kill him when I find out who done this to her." And the sheriff would just say, "We'll find out, R.L. Don't you worry none. Just take care of your wife and the rest of your family."

Small groups of men who had spent the morning searching were now sitting under one of the trees or leaning against the front porch rail. They were pointing and talking among themselves sometimes in a whisper. Sometimes they would get kinda loud until somebody would hush 'em up. They'd say things like, "Bet the Klan's had a hand in this" or "that colored boy, Nathaniel. Never did trust him."

Everything seemed to be in slow motion. Maybe if this day would just end, everything would be all right tomorrow. Finally, the preacher came out on the back porch. I had never seen him without his Sunday-Go-To-Meetin' clothes on afore. He took his big white hankie out and wiped his face before sitting down on the steps between me and Joe. "How you boys doing?" He asked in his most kind voice—not his preachin' voice. "Have you all had anything to eat today?"

We all shook our heads, not knowin' if a sound would come from our mouth.

"I know that this is a hard time for you all. There's a lot goin' on that I'm sure you don't understand. Your mother and father are very upset right now. Just like you all, they're having a hard time dealin' with all this. But they're really lucky to have such a fine family to lean on. And such good kids. I'll go back inside and get one of the ladies to fix you all something to eat," he said as he stood up.

It wasn't long before Rev. Thomas returned to the porch with a plate full of ham biscuits and three glasses of milk.

Joe and Matt nibbled on the warm biscuits but I just wasn't hungry. I took one anyway 'cause Mama would tan my hide if she found out that I was bad-mannered. "Preacher, what happened to our sister?" I finally found the courage to ask.

"Well, boys, sometimes there is meanness in the world that we just can't explain. Seems like Betty was just in the wrong place at the wrong time," he tried to explain.

"She's always been kinda bossy but she wasn't mean or nothin'. She was all the time lookin after animals that was hurt, or takin' care of the ones no one wanted. We didn't fight much. Why did God let this bad thing happen to her? Was He mad at her or somethin? Or is He mad at us?" The things that we all wanted to ask just seemed to spill out of Matt. He sounded just like Betty with all his questions.

"No, boys, God was not mad at Betty. As a matter a fact, He loves her very much. He loves her so much that He needed her to come to heaven and be with Him and He's not mad at you all either," the minister tried to find the words to say. "Lil' Jim, see that Blue Jay feather lying over there on the ground? How about picking it up for me."

I did as I was told. Dusted it off and handed him the bright blue feather with its white tip.

"I'd like to tell you all a story. It's a story about me and my family when I was about the age of Joe here. You see, there were only two children in my family...me and my twin sister, Mary. We lived back in the mountains just like you all do and since there were no other children around, Mary and I were best friends. We did everything together. Sometimes, we would argue and fight just like all brothers and sisters but most of the time we were best buddies." He began to smooth the feather between his fingers as he talked. "But, one day, when she was about twelve, Mary got very sick and had to stay in the bed most of the time. She couldn't run and play anymore. Her bed was next to a window and she would sit for hours and look out the window to see how many birds that she could see in our yard. Mary loved birds. So our Pa made her a birdfeeder and put it on the windowsill so she could see the birds better. After being sick for about a year, Mary died."

Rev. Thomas paused, coughed and cleared his throat before continuing. "I was very sad. I not only had lost my only sister but also my best friend. When we returned home from the funeral, I sat on the side of her bed, looking out the window just like she had done. And there on the windowsill was a beautiful white feather. I think that it was God's way of telling me that He needed one more angel in Heaven and that I will always have a personal angel to watch over me. So every time I see a feather, I know that Mary is close-by, looking after me, and things will work out all right. So you see, guys, you all are very special because not only do you have each other but now you have your own very special angel to look after you. Oh, I know that you will miss her. I still miss Mary and it has been a long time. But every time that you see a feather, you'll know that she's right there looking over you." As he got up to leave, he turned around and handed Matt the blue feather. "Betty's body may be in the house, but she's right out here with you boys."

CHAPTER 18

WHO?

I CAN NEVER REMEMBER GRANNY RUTH sleepin' at our house, but she ain't left ever since Andy went and picked her up. She and Maggie have been doin' most of the cookin and cleanin' and stuff. Lots of other people have been here, too. Just comin' and goin' at all hours. Ladies bringin' food and stuff and settin' it on the table in our kitchen then goin' to Mama and sayin' somethin' real quite. Mama just rocks in her big chair in the corner of the front room. I don't think that she has said a word since that night. She just cries kinda soft and stares out into the room—not like she's lookin' at anything in particular—just lookin'.

Pa comes in once in a while and just kinda looks at her, maybe pats her hand or pulls the shawl around her shoulders, and then goes on back outside to work. It's kinda like if he stays real busy he won't have to dwell much on it.

Sheriff Taylor has been here talkin' to Pa, Daddy Robert, and a bunch of the other men. I heard him ask if Pa had any idea who mighta' done it but Pa just shook his head. Said they's checkin' to see if any strangers had been in town lately or if anybody had seen any hoboes get off the train. No, he didn't have any idea who'd wrote that note and since Robert did what it asked, he didn't think that had anything to do with it. But he'd keep on checkin' about that, too. Went over and talked to Nathaniel and his pa. Somebody said that they had seen him talkin' to Betty a bunch of times down at the store. Most folks in town was pointing a finger his way. But the sheriff just wasn't so sure. Needed some evidence, he said. Ned Putnam told him his son was home all night but he would keep checkin' just to make sure he hadn't snuck out and his folks didn't know. He'd keep his eyes open. Surely somebody would remember seein' something out of the ordinary.

"I just couldn't live with myself if I thought my hirin' on that boy had anything to do with this," I heard Daddy Robert tell Pa as they sat on the front steps after the sheriff left. "Didn't like it, but did just what the note said. Just can't believe the meanness in some folks...doin' this to a little girl who never did nothing but put a smile on people's face." Suddenly, they both got out their white hankie and wiped their face. It was real quite then for a long time and neither one of them seemed to be able to move.

Even Mort was home for the funeral but he could only get a 3-day pass. Told Pa that he'd just stay and be AWOL, what ever that means. But Pa told him to go on, that we could manage. "When you give somebody your word, you gotta keep it. And you done give the Army your word. Ain't no Crawford ever been a quitter and we don't aim to start now."

Big Jack's been here everyday, too. Just shows up and works at what ever needs doin'. I saw the sheriff talkin' to him, too. Don't seem like Big Jack had much to say to him, though. Big Jack don't have much to say to anybody.

We put Betty in the ground up behind Shady Hill Church next to Grandpa Caldwell. His was the only other funeral I've ever been to. It was real scary, but I just kept thinkin' on what the preacher said about angel feathers. Matt picked his guitar and sung *BEULAH LAND*. Betty woulda liked that; it was her favorite. Next to Mama, I guess she was about his biggest fan.

It's been a whole week and we haven't had to go back to school. Granny Ruth says that we'll have to go back on Monday, though. "It's time to get back to doin'. The world don't stop and wait on us. We don't have to stop our grievin' but we gotta grieve while we go through the day." I heard her tell Mama. "Vadie, you got children that need you now and a husband that's hurtin' just as bad as you. It's time to ask the Lord for strength to make it through the day. Then tomorrow, you ask Him again." But Mama just stared at the floor. Granny Ruth shook her head, wiped a tear with the corner of her apron and went back in the kitchen.

"MAMA, WOULD YOU COME IN THE KITCHEN and help me shell out these October beans so they can soak tonight?" Maggie asked rubbing her mother's hand. "They look real good and if we get 'em shelled, we can cook 'em tomorrow," she added as she gently pulled Vadie from her chair and steered her toward the kitchen. "We've got you a spot fixed right here at the table. See, look here at this big basket that Mrs. Medford brought by. We'll shell them out and put them in this dishpan." Vadie calmly did as she was told. She sat in the straight-backed chair but didn't say a word. Maggie gently placed a handful of the beans in Vadie's lap then sat down beside her. She filled her own lap full and began to hum as she took one bean after another, running her fingernail down the length of the brownish pod and emptying out the beans. Granny Ruth busied herself at the sink washing potatoes but keeping a watchful eye on her daughter. She knew that it was important to bring Vadie back into the present quickly or they might loose her forever.

Soon the ping of beans hitting the dishpan could be heard in the small kitchen. Slowly Vadie began to break the long pods open and rake out the contents. It wasn't long before her nimble fingers began to move in a smooth rhythm with the familiar chore and the dishpan began to fill. Maggie and her grandmother chatted noisily about the weather, church, school, and neighbors. Anything that would fill the silence. Each prayed silently that something would work to bring Vadie back from the dark depression that had enveloped her.

BIG JACK HAS BEEN HERE EVERY MORNING already at work when we get up. He only goes home after dark. I overheard Pa tell him more than once, "Don't know how I'll ever pay you, Jack. We'd never have gotten this done without you."

But Jack just shakes his head. "Don't expect nothin'. You'd do the same," he answers, never pausing or looking up from his work.

I carried the hay rakes as Matt led Old Sam toward the barn. It had been a long day, a long week. Our final cut of hay lay in the field ready to be bailed and put into the barn. If it didn't get put up before it rained, it would mildew and be lost. I was so tired, I could hardly put one foot in front of the other and Matt struggled to keep Old Sam moving into the barn.

"Matt, come here." a voice almost whispered.

We both stopped, looking around, not sure where it had come from. "Who was...?"

"Over here, Matt. Come over here, beside the barn," the voice came again, just a little louder.

"Here, Lil' Jim. Stay here. Let me see who it is," Matt ordered as he handed me the bridle and went around the corner. Laying the rakes down, I looped the bridle through the latch on the barn door. Inching my way toward the corner, I had to see what was goin on. Carefully, I lay down and peeked around the boards.

Johnny Lee Hall was holding himself up by leaning against the rough barn siding. He was almost not recognizable with a swollen face and cut lip. His arms and shoulders were stripped with long red marks beneath the gallowses of his overalls.

"Who you been fightin', Johnny Lee?" Matt asked as he reached the beaten figure, not sure what to do.

"Nobody. My pa's done and snapped," he managed to get out before sliding down and sitting on the ground. Matt kneeled beside him. "He done hurt my ma real bad. When I tried to stop him, he took a piece of stove wood to me. He locked Hank and Lem in the barn. Don't know if they's hurt or not."

"Granny Ruth's in the house. I'll go get her. You just stay right here," Matt told him as he quickly stood up and headed toward the house.

"No! Wait, Matt! Don't need no help," he called after him. Matt returned and kneeled beside his friend. "Pa's done gone off up on the mountain. He's probably gone up to his still. Come to tell you somethin, but you can't tell nobody—especially your Pa. Promise?" he groaned, and leaned against the barn. He was having a hard time breathing. I inched closer to try and hear what he was saying. Matt didn't say a word only nodded. "My pa's the one what did that to Betty," he barely whispered.

"Are you sure? How do you know?" was all that Matt could manage to get out. I could not believe my ears and edged nearer to get a better look.

"He was hollerin' at me and Ma and sayin' stuff like 'he fix us like he did that Crawford gal. My Ma's hurt real bad, Matt, and I gotta get back to her afore Pa comes back. But I want you to go to the sheriff. Don't tell your Pa. Just the sheriff. Cause your Pa might try and do somethin' and get hisself in trouble. I'm awful sorry bout what happened to Betty. Your family's always been good to mine what with you and your grandma takin' care of Lem when he got snake bit and all. Don't want no more trouble," he begged as he began to pull himself up. "What was that?" Startled, looking around but not seeing anyone, he managed to stagger to his feet.

I could hardly breathe, so I knew it wasn't me.

"Oh, I don't know. Old Sam probably just kicked over a bucket or somethin." Matt answered absently mindly as he tried to understand what he had just been told. "You sure you don't want Granny Ruth to look at you or maybe go check on your ma?"

"No! Don't want nobody comin' to the house. I'll take care of Ma. Done it afore. It'll just cause more trouble if Pa comes home and finds somebody there," he whispered again trying to steady his feet. "Now remember, Matt, don't tell nobody but the sheriff. Promise?"

"Promise." Matt stammered with a tear streaming down his face. Putting his arm around Johnny Lee, he helped him around the barn and through the gate. "Let me walk part of the way home with you."

"No, I'll be alright."

No one noticed Big Jack as he left the back of the barn and headed off into the woods. No one paid any attention as he headed toward the mountain behind the Hall's and not toward home.

"What are we gonna' do, Matt. What are we gonna' do?" I asked as soon as Matt came back around the corner.

"You heard?" he stammered. "We gotta keep quiet, like Johnny Lee said. Can't tell nobody, you hear Lil' Jim? Nobody." Jerking the bridle loose, he led Sam into the barn. I followed and began hanging the rakes.

"But we gotta tell Pa, Matt. He'll know what to do."

"No!" he almost shouted as he grabbed the front of my overalls. "Johnny Lee's right. Pa'd just go off and try to hurt old man Hall...maybe kill him. Andy, too. What with his temper and all. He'd take a gun and shoot him. You just keep quite, you hear?" Matt ordered as he shook my gallowses. Turnin' me loose, he turned to take care of Old Sam. "Go git Sam some water. I gotta think...figure out a way to go to town and find the sheriff."

"Who was that you was talkin' to, Matt?" Pa asked as he came into the barn.

"Oh, that was just Johnny Lee. His Pa done and beat him up again real bad." Matt answered quickly. Trying to get out of answering any more questions, he began forking hay to Sam while I filled his water trough with the two buckets of water I had carried in from the pump.

Pa took off his hat and wiped the sweat from his brow with his big white hankie. "David Lee must be drinkin' again. But that still ain't no call for him to whip his boy like that. What did he want? Did he need Granny Ruth to see after him?"

"No. Says he'll be fine," Matt tried to think of an excuse. "Just wanted to say he was sorry about Betty and all. Pa, do you think I could go into town after supper?"

"Now what would you be needed to go to town for? It'll be dark soon. Your Mama won't want you to be gone. You just need to stay around here," Pa answered as he stretched his sore back. "Anybody seen Jack? Thought he was in the barn," looking around. "He musta gone on home. You boys get finished up here and come on up to the house. I'm goin' on in and check on your Mama."

As soon as Pa was out of ear shot, I could not help but ask, "How we gonna' tell the sheriff, Matt? You gonna' sneak off tonight and try to find him?"

"Don't know. Maybe the sheriff will be back out here tomorrow. He's been out most every day." Matt answered. "If he don't come by tomorrow night, I'll find a way to sneak off and go to town. But you'd better not say nothing, Lil' Jim, or we'll all be in trouble. Hurry up so we can git to the house afore Pa starts wonderin what we're up to."

CHAPTER 19

ANOTHER MURDER?

IT WAS BARELY NOON when the sheriff's car pulled up in the driveway. We were sittin on the back porch finishin up our sandwiches and Maggie was gatherin the empty plates. "Afternoon, R.L. Looks like you boys been workin' real hard," the sheriff commented as he got out of his car and went over to shake R.L.'s hand. "You about to get that hay up?"

"It'll be in by dark if we keep at it," Pa answered taking the last swallow from the big glass of milk. "What brings you this way?"

"Got ourself some trouble down at the Hall place. Hazel and the boys done found David Lee dead this mornin'," the sheriff answered, looking at each of the Crawfords for a knowing sign. "Seems he didn't come home last night and when Johnny Lee went out to the woodshed this mornin', he found him." No one breathed. You could hear a penny drop.

"What happened? Heart attack or somethin'?" Pa asked trying to figure out why the sheriff would be involved and why he would come to tell them about David Lee dying.

"Nope. Got hisself killed, I reckon," Sheriff Taylor told them as he took off his hat and run his fingers through his hair. He looked at Andy. "Any of you see David Lee yesterday?"

"No sir. We ain't seen him in a long time. We ain't been off the farm except to go to Betty's funeral in over a week." Andy was quick to answer. "What would anybody be wantin' to kill old David Lee for anyway?"

"His boy, Johnny Lee, was down at the barn last night talkin' to Matt. Said his Pa had done and beat him up again. Ain't that right, Matt?" Pa told the sheriff still puzzled.

"Yeah. He was hurt real bad." Matt quickly answered, not knowing if he should share the secret now or not. I eased over toward Matt trying not to look at the sheriff, afraid he would ask me something.

"Is Johnny Lee all right? Why didn't you come and get me or Granny Ruth? Is he hurt bad? Why hadn't you told me?" Maggie worriedly asked her brother.

"He said not to. Said he'd be all right." Matt answered her, stepping back and wanting to go to the barn so he could think.

"R.L., let's me and you take a walk around to the front of the house. How about Big Jack, he around?" Sheriff Taylor asked, putting his hat back on and shuffling his feet.

"Yeah, he's down at the barn." Pa stood up, handed his glass to Maggie, and followed the sheriff as they made their way around the house toward the front porch.

"What do you reckon that's all about?" Andy quickly asked the others as soon as they got out of earshot. "Why old man Hall probably got drunk and fell down and broke his neck or somethin'. Probably wasn't killed at all. Maybe Johnny Lee and his brothers got tired of him beatin' up on 'em and killed him theirself," he speculated.

"Johnny Lee wouldn't kill nobody, Andy. Don't you go and talk like that." Maggie scolded her brother. "You should have told me he was hurt, Matt. You should have told me." But Matt didn't hear her. He had slipped off the porch and was heading toward the barn to think.

I quietly opened the back door and sneaked into the front sitting room so I could try and hear what the sheriff had to say. I put my ear to the front window and peaked through the curtains.

"R.L., I wanted to talk to you alone 'cause I got somethin' to tell you and I think it would be best if you told the rest of your family," the sheriff began as they got to the front steps. "Don't hardly know how to say this, so I'm just sayin' it straight out. Hazel told me that David Lee was the one that killed Betty."

R.L. went to one knee. Had he stumbled or fainted or what. "How'd she know?" he finally managed to ask, still on his knee with his head bowed afraid to look up.

"Well, it seems that David Lee beat up on her and the boys real bad yesterday. Johnny Lee tried to stop him and he took a piece of wood to him. Seems David Lee told Hazel and Johnny that he might just do to them what he did to Betty. Then he left and went up the mountain. They didn't see him again until Johnny found him this morning," Sheriff Taylor explained. "Hazel said that she didn't know nothin' until yesterday."

"And David Lee's dead?" R.L. asked not believing what he had heard. The sheriff nodded his head looking the first suspect right in the eye. "And somebody killed him? Who do you think? Surely, you don't think me or the boys woulda done it."

"I don't know who done it. Maybe somebody got mad about his liquor or something. I don't know. Guess I'll have to find out though," he answered, helping R.L. to his feet. "You sure you and your boys didn't know and take matters in your own hands?"

"How can you even think that, Sheriff? We are mad about what happened to Betty but we ain't no killers." R.L. answered him jerking away from his helping hand.

"Do you want me to be around when you tell your family?" the sheriff asked as they started toward the back of the house.

"No, I'll do it. Gotta be careful with Vadie. She's still not herself." R.L. could still not believe his ears. "Maybe Johnny Lee and his brothers killed him. Maybe they got tired of being beat on."

"Yeah. That's what I thought at first, too. But it took somebody might strong to do to David Lee what was done and Johnny Lee done got broke ribs and probably a broke arm from that piece of wood his Pa hit him with. I left him over at Doc Prichard's. He wouldn't have been able to do it even with his brothers help and they were beat up pretty bad, too."

"Why, what do you mean? What was done to David Lee?" R.L. could not help but ask as they started toward the back porch.

"Somebody done wrapped him up in barbed wire. Head to foot. His head was busted in with a big rock, too. Weren't a pretty sight," he reluctantly told him. "Oh, I almost forgot. I believe this mighta belonged to Betty," he added as he removed a small gold locket from his pocket and handed it to R.L. "Found it in David Lee's overall pocket. Found these in his pocket, too." The sheriff placed three "Best of Show" tags in R.L.'s hand. "Sorry, I didn't have the time to hunt for your dog when she went missin'. Thought she mighta just run off. Maybe if I had looked into that a little closer, this might not have happened to Betty."

"You can't blame yourself, Sheriff. Ain't nobody's fault that David Lee Hall was a mean man. Heck, if I had of knowed, I'd of give him all of them pups," R.L. told him as he gripped the only things he had left of two of the loves of his life. Tucking them all securely in his pocket, he took a deep breath as he tried to compose himself before facing his family.

I had to find Matt. The sheriff knows. We don't have to tell. Running through the house, I pushed the back screen so hard it almost came off it's hinges. "Where's Matt? Where's Matt?"

"I don't know. He musta went to the barn. What's wrong with you?" Andy asked. "You see a spook or something?"

But I didn't stop, didn't even slow down. "Matt! Matt! Where are you, Matt?"

Chapter 20

November 1949—Gettin' on with Things

IT'S BEEN MORE THAN A MONTH since Betty died and David Lee Hall was found. The sheriff has been out to the farm at least once a week. Just askin' questions and looking around and stuff. Andy told Pa that he thought the sheriff must think it musta been us what killed David Lee—with his comin' out so often. But Pa said, "It's just the sheriff's job to look into things. Can't leave no stone unturned." Pa didn't tell him he was right, that the sheriff thought it might have been us.

But it shore seems like the sheriff ain't never gonna' find out who done it. I heard him tell Pa one day, "Ain't got no clues. They was a mighty lot of people who didn't take a liking to David Lee…the way he treated his family and all. But don't know nobody that wanted to kill him. Found out he sold whiskey to some fellers over Asheville way but none of them has been around these parts in a spell. Reckon I'll just have to keep on looking."

Nathaniel left Hazelgrove right after Betty died. Moved to Atlanta or someplace. Daddy Robert said Ned and Susie cried when they put him on the bus that morning in front of the store. But the Sit 'n Spit Club fellers just whispered to each other, "Good riddance." as the bus pulled away.

Mama's been doin better, too. Granny Ruth stopped spending the night and doin the cookin and cleanin about two weeks back. I heard her tell Mama, "Vadie, the Lord is doin His part to get us all through this. Now it's time for us to do ours."

Mama still rocks in her chair and cries sometimes but Granny Ruth said that was alright when I asked her about it. Matt told mama the Preacher's story about the angel feather and I think it made her feel better cause she keeps a feather in her apron pocket all the time.

Pa put them three "Best of Show" tags on the table next to the carved dog. Said it was our way of showin respect.

We've all gone back to school. Even the Hall boys are back. They come every day now. Some folks whisper and say things like they shouldn't be there what with their Pa bein a murderer and all. But I don't reckon it's their fault that their Pa was so mad all the time. Daddy Robert says, "Can't hold the sons responsible for the sins of the father." Reckon that's the way I see it, too.

Heard Lem say that Big Jack just showed up at their house one morning right after their Pa was killed. Started doin most of the chores and told their ma, "These young 'uns need to be in school. Won't never amount to nothin if they don't get some learnin. As long as they go, I'll do what needs doin around here. They can help out in the mornings and when they get home."

Seems the first thing Big Jack did was make them boys show him where David Lee's moonshine still was. Then, one afternoon, they all got shovels, axes, and stuff, and went up on the mountain and chopped down that still. Even Miz Hall. Piled it all up, poured out the whiskey, and set it all afire. Lem said it sure was some sight. Flames reachin' as high as the tree tops. Said his ma just sat on a big rock and laughed. First time he had heard her laugh in a long time, he said.

Lem said that his ma told him, "Jack, you made these boys go back to school and that was good and I thank ye for it. But we need to go back to church, too. Don't know if I can go it alone."

"Reckon, I could go," Jack had answered, "Been awhile." Low and behold, that next Sunday morning, he was there, waitin on the porch.

They sat on the back pew all together, even Big Jack. Didn't have his army clothes on either. Had on regular stuff and even had his hair all combed and slicked back. I ain't never seen Big Jack at church afore and I ain't never seen him in nothing but his army clothes. Why, I wasn't even sure if that was even him.

After church when Mama caught Miz Hall out in the churchyard and told her what she thought, seems like everything got better. Mama's back to bein Mama again...yellin at me to git a hustle on, and do this or that. But I guess she orders everybody around, even Pa. She had Maggie gatherer up all of Betty's clothes and take 'em down to the Young's house. Said they had plenty of use for 'em with all their passel of young 'uns. She still has a hard time going into Betty's room, though. I can tell. It's hard for me, too. I even miss Betty's bossin me around.

The Halls and Big Jack came back to church the next Sunday, too. They didn't sneak in and sit on the back row, no sir. Sit right there in their own pew. Folks don't have as much to say now, either. Now, I don't mean that they are askin Miss Hall how's she doin or what a pretty frock she has on or nothing. But at least they ain't whisperin and sayin things like, "What are they doin here?" and stuff. Reckon they figured that if Mama could make her peace with 'em, that they ought to, too.

Preacher says, "The Lord don't want us to hate. Wants us to love our neighbor." Well, I don't know much about that. I got the not hating part down pretty good, but I don't know about that love your neighbor part. Joe told me that Sarah Young's been bragging to the other girls that I'm her boyfriend and she loves me...but I shore don't love her, neighbor or not!

www.ingramcontent.com/pod-product-compliance
Lightning Source LLC
Chambersburg PA
CBHW020432180626
46812CB00003B/1202